SWEET TEA

QUILTING BEE

THE SOUTHERN GRACE SERIES

GLENDA C. MANUS

Library of Congress Cataloging-in-Publication
Data is on file with the publisher

Text copyright © 2017 by Glenda Manus
Published in 2017 by South Ridge Press
ISBN-13: 978-1542896955
ISBN-10: 1542896959

Printed in the United States of America
24 23 22 21 20 19 18 17 16

Interior and Cover Designer: Greg Banks
Front and back photos by: Cherie Steele

First Original Edition

This is a work of fiction. Any resemblance to any actual
person, living or dead, business establishments, events or
locales is strictly coincidental.

A special thank you to my editors, Laura Whittaker and Krista Cook, for their keen observations and helpful suggestions.

To my husband, who is not averse to cooking and washing dishes when I'm glued to my computer on good writing days.

To my friends and family for their encouragement and prayers.

To the Osceola United Methodist Church Quilters who let me hang around and soak up information.

To Betty G, the one-of-a-kind postmistress whose personality shines through the fictional Betty, of Park Place Post Office fame.

To Betty Broome, a friend whose quilting skills are evident in the 'Jewelry Box' quilt she made featured on the front cover. The Sunbonnet Sue quilt, also featured on the cover, was made by a family member of another friend, Pat Oglesby.

To Cherie Steele Photography for the front cover photo and the author bio photo on the back cover. Another talented lady!

To my readers, who tell me they feel comfortable with my characters and would love to call Park Place home.

And to God, the One who gives me strength, and whose grace is sufficient.

Isaiah 40:31

"But those who hope in the Lord will renew their strength. They will soar on wings like eagles; they will run and not grow weary, they will walk and not be faint."

CHAPTER 1

TALL AND SLIM

Wanda Burns made a mad dash for the door of the Park Place Post Office and stepped inside. A bright blue plastic grocery bag covered her head with the handles tied loosely around her neck. She put her package on the counter and untied the bag, shaking the water out on the floor. "What a mess of a weather forecast. I thought it was supposed to be sunny and warm today, and here we get this rain that makes the ducks go into hiding." She gave the bag one more shake, then looked up to find Betty's evil eye settled upon her. "It's true. The pair of wood ducks on Fox's Pond were nowhere to be seen when I passed by and they're always out there." Betty continued her glare from behind the counter. "What?" Wanda said. "What did I say?"

"It's not what you said, it's what you did. Don't go shakin' that water all over my floor. Don't you know wet floors are a safety hazard. Now I'll have to put out that yellow wet floor sign so we don't have any lawsuits on our hands. Hmph!"

Wanda put her hands on her hips. "Betty! There's not enough water on that bag to drown a flea. Why are you so grumpy anyway?"

Betty reached under the counter, producing a roll of paper towels and tore one off. "This weather's enough to make anyone grumpy. Here, take this and wipe it up, will you?"

"Yes Ma'am!" Wanda dropped the paper towel on the floor and rubbed it with her shoe, then picked it up and threw it in the trash can.

"That's better," Betty said.

Rain was beating furiously on the window pane and tender sprigs from the newly leafed trees in town were blowing across Main Street. Almost everyone in town was watching out their windows as the March storm lashed out. At the height of the storm, a lone figure in a hooded raincoat was seen hunched over and walking toward the dumpster in the alleyway across from the post office beside May's Flower Shop.

Wanda had come by to mail a package, but at the loud clap of thunder, she squealed. "Thunderstorms scare me half to death", she said and walked over to the window, looking out. "For heaven's sake, what would possess Kathleen Crowder to take her trash out during this storm?"

Betty had gone back behind the counter to scan a package for Liz Clark, the Presbyterian preacher's wife, but Wanda's exclamation got her curiosity up. Dropping the package back down on the scales, she stopped what she was doing and walked out from behind the counter to take a peak. She looked in the direction where Wanda was pointing. "No, that's too tall for Kathleen," she said, "and it's not Kathleen's raincoat. She has a red one. That raincoat's black, and look, it has gray trim around the hood and the sleeves."

"How the heck can you see the color of the trim from here. I can barely tell it's black."

"You need to get your cataracts done like I did. I can see a fly on a camel's back from fifty yards away."

"Betty, stop that. You've probably never even seen a camel."

"Yes ma'am, I have! I saw one just last Christmas in the manger scene over at that Baptist Church in Waxhaw." She grinned. "But I was stretching things a mite. It was December and the flies weren't out, but if they were I would have seen one."

Wanda looked over at Liz who was about to laugh and sighed, shaking her head. Betty kept right on looking out the window. "I think that might be Sam Owens from The Banty Hen Antique Shop. But why's he stooping over like that. He's usually ramrod straight."

"Maybe to keep the wind out of his face," Wanda said.

Liz followed them to see what the commotion was all about. She saw the hooded figure and shivered. It wasn't anyone she knew. The grim reaper, she thought to herself.

Across the street at Crowder's Feed and Seed, Kathleen Crowder looked out and said to her husband, "Good grief, Junie! May Williams is rambling around out there at the dumpster behind her flower shop in this weather. Doesn't she know she could catch pneumonia, or worse, be struck dead by lightning?"

Junie's eyes were still dilated from his eye doctor appointment earlier that morning, but he squinted and looked out anyway. "I cain't see a dad-burned thing, Kathleen. I'm blind as a bat until these eye drops wear off."

Larry Braswell had come in to buy chicken feed and was waiting out the storm. He stepped over to the front window and peered out. "I don't think that's May, Kathleen - too thin. Maybe it's Valerie Owens from the antique shop. She's tall and slim."

"No, Valerie's not that tall and she's not crazy either. She would send Sam out to the dumpster if she needed to throw something away bad enough to go outside in this weather. And it couldn't be Sam - he's thicker around the middle."

At the same time, May Williams peeked her head out the back door of her flower shop to see if the rain had let up. She needed to make a delivery to the hospital where Angie Edwards had been blessed with a new baby boy, but that could wait another hour or so. She and the baby were staying overnight anyway since she'd had a c-section. No siree, she wasn't going out in this weather! A tall, gangly man in a dark raincoat with the hood pulled tightly around his head was cutting through the alley and heading in the direction of the candy store's back entrance. Or was it a woman? No, she was pretty sure it was a man, but he was awfully skinny. Maybe it was the new man working behind the lunch counter at Carter's. She had heard he was tall - and thin too according to Clara Carter. Clara had pestered May to let her arrange a blind date with him, but May had said, hunh-unh, if she ever found herself a man, it would be of her own choosing. She called out the back door at the retreating figure, "Hey! Are you crazy! You better get yourself out of this storm." But the wind carried her voice in the opposite direction. It was blowing so hard, it shut the door right in her face.

The tall, thin person, man or woman, nobody knew, was seen by at least a half dozen people in town that morning, but following the events of the next morning, not a one of them remembered to tell about it. If the merchants on Main had realized they had seen a murderer in their midst, they would have paid closer attention.

***

"In like a lion, out like a lamb." Rock Clark was talking, and even though ten-month old Matthew couldn't understand a word, he paid rapt attention. His blue eyes searched the eyes of his daddy, seemingly thrilled that he was speaking to him, the only other person in the room. He reached up to touch Rock's face and giggled. "That's what they say about the month of March, Matthew. Did you know that?"

They were sitting on the window seat in the church office watching the rain lash against the window panes. From his position, he could normally see the manse on the other side of the parking lot, and the church behind it. Today he could barely see fifty feet in front of him. The Japanese Maple and the flowering crabapple tree planted right outside the window were bent double. The crabapple tree had been filled with blooms but the harsh wind was stripping them off. The ground underneath it was covered in a soft pink carpet of blossoms. He suddenly heard a loud popping noise and looked far to the left in time to see the huge oak tree in the courtyard give up one of its large limbs to the storm. It just missed the water fountain, the one with the angel holding its arms heavenward. The fountain was made of marble and had been donated to the church by a wealthy congregant long before Rock came to Park Place. If something happened to it, it would cost a fortune to replace. Rock looked heavenward, just like the angel, and spoke quietly.

"*Thank you, Lord, for shielding our angel from the falling tree branch. I pray that you will calm the storm's fury and spread your loving arms over our town to keep everyone safe. I ask that you protect Liz as she's running her errands. I offer you praise, Lord, for it is your awesome power that gives us sunshine and rain to nourish our crops that provide for our physical needs, and your Holy Spirit that provides for our spiritual needs and gives us everlasting life. In the name of your Son, Jesus Christ, I pray. Amen.*"

When he looked up, his baby boy laughed and clapped his hands as if he was applauding the prayer. He picked him up from the window seat, and held him close, nuzzling his neck and taking in the sweet baby smell. He added a few words to his prayer. "*PS God, one more thing. Thank you for the greatest blessing of all, for bringing Liz into my life and this gift that I hold in my arms, our Matthew...our son.*"

He loosened his hold on the squirming baby who was fast outgrowing the need to be cuddled. He was a curious child and when Rock perched him back on the window seat, he turned once again to the window, beating on it with the palm of his hand. His soft blonde hair was curled in ringlets and Rock was inclined to agree with Liz, that it was too cute to cut anytime soon.

Liz brought their boy to the office over an hour earlier so she could go grocery shopping and run errands. Reva entertained him for a while until he fell asleep in his playpen in front of her desk. When the weather alert had sounded on Rock's smartphone calling for severe thunderstorms, he had urged Reva to go home. He planned to do the same, but by the time he woke Matthew up and was ready to open the door and make a mad dash for the manse, the storm broke loose forcing them to stay inside.

Suddenly a lightning bolt lit up the sky with a clap of thunder right on its heels. It startled Matthew and he began to cry. "Come on, big boy," he said as he hurriedly lifted him from the window seat. "We can't sit close to the window when it's lightning." He bounced him up in the air and Matthew started laughing again, one of those infectious laughs that always sent him and Liz in stitches. He loved the sound of his laughter.

His thoughts drifted to just two short years earlier. At forty-four, he thought he was pretty content living the life of a bachelor, but there was always a nagging little thought that something was missing. He was the pastor of the small, but growing Presbyterian church whose office he sat in now. His congregants loved and respected him and he loved them in return. His greatest joy was preaching God's word and he tried his best to practise what he preached, although he sometimes fell short. His only real heartache at that time was that he had lost his closest friend the year before. Ron Logan had died of a heart attack at forty-five and Rock took it upon himself to help Ron's widow through her grief, as he was grieving right along with her. Their feelings for each other, even though they fought it, deepened from friendship to a different kind of love and eighteen months after Ron passed away, Rock proposed, Liz accepted and just ten short months later, little Matthew was born. This is what he'd been missing all along.

The wind and rain had not let up and Matthew was beginning to get fussy. "Don't worry, Matthew, we don't need to go anywhere. Your mommy left a stash of the good stuff in the refrigerator for you and I've got Reva's chocolate chip cookies to tide me over. We won't go hungry."

Holding his son with his left arm, he opened the door of the fridge with his right, pulling out a bottle of milk from the bottom rack. He stuck it in the microwave for a few seconds and then shook it, testing the temperature on his arm. "Just right," he said. Matthew was practically jumping out of his arm to get to the bottle. "Wait, don't get greedy. Your daddy needs a cookie."

He picked up the platter of cookies off the counter in one hand, balancing the baby in the other. He set the platter on the small table beside a rocking chair Reva had brought to the office with the excuse that her grandchildren were too big to be rocked, and then sat down holding Matthew on his lap. Rock had to admit, the rocker had come in handy. Reva loved to sit rocking Matthew when Liz did housecleaning or ran errands. He picked up a cookie and started nibbling on it which only made the baby fuss louder and start crying.

"Here ya go, have at it," he said, putting the bottle in the wide-open mouth, "but you can't have a cookie. Your momma will have my hide if I give you chocolate." Matthew latched onto the bottle greedily, finally content. Rock watched in amusement as the bottle was quickly being drained of its contents. He finally slowed down and even though he was fighting to stay awake, his little eyes grew heavy. His soft, fine eyelashes fluttered a few times and he went to sleep, still sucking on the bottle. "Wake up, silly boy," Rock said, jiggling the bottle back and forth in his mouth. He repeated his efforts several times until the bottle was empty, then took it away. His own heart fluttered much like Matthew's eyelashes had done. The love he felt for this precious little life in his arms was too much to describe. He once again breathed in the sweet baby scent and put his head back against the rocker, content to daydream for a while.

That was how Liz found them an hour later, long after the storm had passed. She smiled at Rock's rhythmic breathing, giving in to an occasional snore. Matthew's right arm had relaxed to the point that it was dangling through the arm of the rocker. As she gazed down at the two of them, her heart was full. She put her hand out to touch Matthew's curls and Rock awakened with a jerk. "I'm sorry, I didn't mean to startle you," she said.

"Was I asleep?" he asked.

"Out like a light," she said, laughing at his puzzled expression. She reached over and pulled Matthew's arm back through the arm of the rocker and placed it on his tummy.

"Did you get through running your errands? I was worried about you."

"Most of them. I had to stay in the post office for a while until it quit raining, but Betty entertained me."

"I'll bet," he said, his eyes twinkling.

Her expression changed to one of worry. "Rock, in the middle of that storm, there was this tall, grim looking figure walking from the street to the alleyway behind May's Flower Shop. I felt the oddest sensation, like something dark and sinister was about to happen."

"Maybe we should call May to see if she's okay," he said.

"She is," Liz said. "When I was leaving the post office, she was out front sweeping leaves from the sidewalk that had blown off the trees. Maybe the creepy feeling was just my imagination running wild because of the dismal rain." She reached down and kissed him, then kissed the sweet little face of the child lying in his arms. "See, I feel better already," she said. She kissed him again, this time lingering just a little bit longer. "It's amazing how being with the two people I love best in all the world helps put things in perspective."

"Hmm, let's try that again," he said, and pulled her down once more for her lips to meet his.

CHAPTER 2

REVIVE US AGAIN

"Sam, did you take the good pen off my desk again?"

"Yes, dear, but I put it back. Look in the desk drawer."

"Oh, here it is. Sorry, I should have looked before I accused you." Valerie Owens sat in a straight back chair and squirmed uncomfortably. It hadn't yet occurred to her that her plush office chair had been moved and the antique monstrosity she now sat in was taking its place. Her elbows were propped upon the old oak desk in the musty back room of one of Park Place's oldest buildings, built in 1892 as a general store. It had once been owned and occupied by one of the town's founding fathers, Oscar Leo Yoder, a descendent of German immigrants who had moved much farther South than their relatives who had stopped and settled in Pennsylvania. Advertising his goods as "general merchandise" was appropriate since he carried just about anything a person would need in the nearby farming and textile communities. An 1894 newspaper clipping from the Park Place Gazette was under the glass that topped the oak desk where Valerie sat. It advertised a big sale. A Homer Young Sewing Machine for $18.50, W. L. Douglas shoes for gentlemen for $3.00, men's and women's hats for $2.50, a side of beef at 12 cents per pound, a blacksmith anvil for a mere $1.00, and pine coffins conveniently located on the second floor for $14 each. There was a small advertisement right below the general store ad that offered midwife services for $4. Valerie's husband's running joke was that it had been cheaper back then to bring a body into the world than to take one out. Valerie thought it a lame joke, but most people laughed, and then Sam would say, "it's not that much different nowadays, is it?", and some of the old-timers would comment that they wished they could be buried in one of those old pine coffins like they made back in the day and what a waste it was for all those newfangled metal caskets and concrete vaults to be underground holding a body that should be going nature's way of dust to dust. Valerie didn't voice her wishes to be cremated, because it seemed to be a taboo subject in this neck of the woods. Most people would look at you like you were going to hell in a handbasket if you mentioned the word cremation. She figured that eventually the consensus would change when land got too expensive to bury people who in afterlife wouldn't care one way or another.

She put down her pen and closed the ledger book. Her thoughts were getting too morbid. Besides, she was sick of trying to get the numbers to come out in the black instead of the stubborn red that spoke of aging baby boomers, the avid collectors of yesteryear, who were now downsizing instead of buying more stuff. The younger generation was going with the trend of minimalism versus clutter and Valerie was afraid the antique business would soon be a thing of the past, an antiquated obsession. She smiled at her own play of words. Antiques had become quite an obsession for them when she and Sam retired and moved into the old Harper House in town. Trying to fill the Victorian home with period furniture was their starting point and it just escalated from there. As they bid against other people at estate auctions, it was apparent that in those days they weren't the only ones obsessed with buying antiques. It was the thrill of the hunt that sucked them in and it never let them go. She squirmed in her seat again, then noticed the chair. Her comfortable office chair was clear across the room at Sam's desk.

"That stinker!" she said aloud. "Surely he doesn't think he can fool me when he changes chairs." She swapped chairs and while doing so noticed how heavy and cumbersome the old chair was. There was no wonder he kept stealing hers. Poor dear, she thought, and him with a bad back!

Opening the antique store when they retired was a way to help finance their obsession. She and Sam didn't depend on the shop for a living. They opened *The Banty Hen Antique Shop* as a hobby, each having a decent retirement income from past careers. But now her keen business sense told her that they couldn't keep losing money. It would squander away their nest egg eventually. Over the years, the store had seen many merchants come and go but it never stood empty long. The last establishment within these walls had been a jewelry store, and she and Sam grabbed up the lease as soon as they heard Hayes Jewelers was moving to the new mall in Sparta.

Changes, hmm.... Recently she had been mulling around in her mind something to add to the store to bring in more interest and if they were lucky, more income. Just yesterday, a new customer came in asking about antique quilts. When Valerie showed her the few quilts in the shop, the woman spoke her disappointment.

"That's not what I had in mind," she'd said brusquely. "That's a paltry little lot of quilts, none of them really what I consider antique." She seemed awfully put out.

Valerie explained to her that in small Southern communities where most residents have lived out their entire lives, quilts are handed down through the generations and families treasure them, sometimes displaying them and sometimes packing them away in old cedar trunks for the next generation to treasure. More often though, they've been used so many times they're threadbare. It was a rare thing to find a nice heirloom quilt in local estate sales. Most of the quilts in the shop were from picking trips she and Sam had made to Pennsylvania's Amish Country.

One of Valerie's regular customers from the Sun's Up Retirement Village was shopping in the store and overheard the conversation. Her look was incredulous at the tone of voice the other customer was using.

"I agree, Valerie," she said, ignoring the other woman. "I've never understood how people can store away the beautiful things their ancestors made in a trunk. It's better to use or display them and feel the love and warmth that was put into the making of them."

Valerie gave her a warm smile. "I'm glad you understand."

"Quilting does seem to be a dying artform though, don't you think? Someday all the old quilts will be gone and new generations will be left without the comfort of handmade quilts. It would be nice if there was a quilter's club in town. I'd love to join one."

Valerie asked why she hadn't joined the quilting guild at Sun's Up. She knew they had one. "I checked into it, but what I'd really like to find is a club with local women, a good old-fashioned quilting bee", she had said. "This is a new adventure for us. If we'd wanted to continue living life as we always have, we would've stayed where we were. What's the use of moving to the South if we don't blend in and make new friends with the locals?"

Valerie had found it refreshing to hear this attitude and felt an instant connection with her. She tried to recall her name; Kay, yes, that was it.

The other woman had an arrogant, condescending air about her that Valerie found hard to ignore. "Hmph! I still can't believe you don't have a large inventory of quilts."

Valerie stared at her. Had the lady not been listening to a thing she said? "Ma'am, this is a small town. What would I do with such a large inventory?" The minute she said it, she realized how rude she sounded, but the woman was getting on her nerves. As with most rude people, she didn't seem to notice and continued to talk.

"Antique quilts, that's the only kind I'm interested in. Especially the old appliqued designs. Do you ever get any of those?" When Valerie didn't answer, she said brusquely, "I'll check back. I'm visiting someone and won't be here long."

The whole time the woman was speaking, Valerie couldn't take her eyes off the small birthmark near her hairline. It was a perfectly shaped heart. Valerie offered to call her if something came in, but the woman left in a huff.

After she left, Kay shook her head. "What was that all about? I don't usually make snap judgments of people, but she was rude."

Valerie shrugged her shoulders. "I wish I knew," was all she said. She didn't want her new friend to think she talked about her customers. She wrote down Kay's phone number and promised that she would ask around about a local quilting club.

She had followed up on her promise and called Lydia Swanson, a quilter from church, and found out that the nearest quilting club was in Sparta and it was bursting at the seams with members. After talking to Lydia, the little seed Kay had planted inside Valerie's head took sprout. Lydia agreed Park Place was ripe for a quilting club. Apparently quilting was all the rage now and the little seed was beginning to grow into a full-scale plan. She and Sam had discussed it over breakfast, and now that he had given his approval, she planned to call on a few of the local quilters who had to go all the way to Sparta to quilt. If they were receptive, she would start a new club right here in the store. One of the side rooms in the shop was currently being used as a year-round Christmas section and could easily be turned into a quilting room. They could quilt away to their heart's content, and she might even join them. Learning new things would keep her mind alert, not that she was old enough to worry about things like that yet. She was still young at heart and didn't consider herself even remotely old with a mere sixty-seven years behind her.

She could picture it now. She would recruit Sam to make a rustic sign to go over the door introducing *The Banty Hen Quilter's Club*.

Yes! This was a good plan. She would carry a line of quilting supplies and would even offer to sell on consignment some of the things the quilters made. It would be a nice drawing card. Valerie unplugged the only fixture in the office that wasn't an antique, her laptop, and carried it into the furniture section of the store. She needed to make a list of all the things she needed to do and number one on the list would be to ask Lydia to come by the shop soon and help get an order together. It was raining outside so it was a perfect day to relax and do some research. Until the rain went away, very few people would get out and about on Main Street. She sat down on her favorite chair, an old Eastlake rocker, recently re-upholstered in burgundy velvet, and opened the laptop. She quickly connected to the WiFi and typed in "wholesale quilting supplies" in the search engine. As Google fed her the list of options, she started singing the refrain of an old hymn, one that put her in mind of the project she was about to undertake that she hoped would change the dynamics of the shop and put them into the black again. Her rich soprano voice lifted high into the old building and echoed off the walls.

"Hallelujah, thine the glory.
Hallelujah, amen;
Hallelujah, thine the glory,
Revive us again."

CHAPTER 3

THE STRANGER

Valerie was so lost in her song that she didn't hear Sam come up behind her. "Sounds like a choir of angels in here," he said. "You only sing when you've got something up your sleeve."

"Lord have mercy, Sam. You scared me half to death." She looked up from the computer. Sam's eyes were twinkling as he looked down at her. She smiled. She loved this man she had been married to for almost forty-five years. Twenty-five years ago, she wouldn't have given their marriage a snowball in July chance of making it another year. They had each been so involved in their separate careers, and had lost whatever spark that had kindled their romance during their first years of marriage. If it hadn't been for her aging parents and Sam's parents collaborating with each other and begging them to at least give marriage counseling a try, she was sure they would have gone their separate ways, but Sam's father arranged for them to meet with a Christian marriage counselor. It had been nothing short of a miracle.

Early on, they had both drifted away from their faith with the excuse that Sunday was their only day to rest and church was just too time-consuming. Within months of meeting with Dr. Lucas, they renewed their wedding vows and renewed their commitment to an all-knowing God who had not given up on them, even though they had turned their backs on Him. Since then, Sunday worship was an integral part of their lives and in turn, each day brought a newness of spirit to their marriage.

"I didn't mean to frighten you," Sam said. Then he leaned over and whispered, pointing to the front of the store. "But I thought you may be more frightened if the strange customer who walked in just a few minutes ago made his way back here and startled you."

"And why would he do that?"

"You'll see," he said. "Come on, we'll walk to the front together."

"I can't believe someone ventured out in this weather." When she got to the front, it was all she could do to keep from gasping. The man was strange indeed. His unkempt appearance and slouchy posture was bad enough, but the piercing black eyes and the Albert Einstein shock of gray hair sprouting out in all directions when he took off his rain hat was even more disconcerting. Mentally measuring his size, she decided he was almost as thick around the middle as he was tall. He was a good four inches shorter than Sam; 5'6", maybe. Sam was 5'10". She plastered her best smile across her face. After all, it isn't appearance that makes a man, it's what's inside. Hadn't that been the subject of many lessons on compassion that she had learned over the years?

"Is there something we can help you with?" She glanced to her left to make sure Sam was still by her side. He put his arm on her shoulder.

"Are you looking for some sort of treasure today?" Sam asked. "Maybe something for yourself, or a friend? As you can see, we have a shop full of interesting things."

Sam continued to ramble on. She could tell he was just as befuddled as she was by the old guy's appearance, and they both watched as puddles formed on the newly waxed heart-pine floor from his dripping wet raincoat. The only thing dry about him seemed to be the brown wool scarf that was wrapped snugly around his neck. She found herself hoping that the man would spout off something clever. Maybe he was just a quirky scholarly type, too caught up in his own genius to care about his appearance. After all, he did have Einstein's hair, but when he spoke, she knew she was wrong. His voice was rough and wheezy and whatever he said was so muffled, she couldn't understand a thing. She wished he hadn't spoken at all because he had the breath of a thousand camels. She couldn't help but wrinkle up her nose and take a step backwards. It was then that she saw he held a large plastic bag in his hand and it made her uneasy to think what could be inside it. After a brief coughing spell, he finally seemed to find his voice.

"I'm sorry," he said, still a little wheezy but at least she understood him. "I've been sick and I know I must look a sight."

She nodded. "I'm so sorry, I hope you're recovering. What can we help you with today?"

He put the bag on the floor and they both looked on with trepidation as he opened it. Water was dripping from the bag, but surprisingly the contents didn't look wet. He shook the bag and more droplets of water pooled on the floor.

"I came to see if you wanted to buy this quilt. It's old and valuable." He carefully pulled it out of the bag, handling it like a mother would a newborn baby. He started to unfold it. "Where can I put it so you can see the full quilt?" he asked. "I don't want it to get wet." He was back to wheezing again. She really didn't want to see anything he had in that bag, but then a wave of compassion came over her. Whatever could this poor man have been through to get in this kind of condition?

She moved toward the glass counter that held their mid-century costume jewelry. "Here," she said, "you can spread it out on the counter." She picked up a small dinner bell and a calling card holder from the countertop and put them underneath on the shelf below. He shuffled to the counter and started unfolding the large piece of fabric. This time when she gasped, it wasn't at a ghastly appearance, but at one of the most beautiful quilt designs she had ever seen. She had no doubts of the authenticity of the quilt. Even with her limited experience in identifying the age of textiles, there was just no way the look and feel of it could have been replicated. The quilt was made up of blocks and each block had been elaborately appliqued with a different design. The colors were vibrant but in a soft muted kind of way.

"It's lovely," she said, staring at it in amazement. "Wherever did it come from?"

It was the first time she had even seen a hint of a smile as he looked upon it with pride. "It's old," he said, "very old."

"Do you know its history?" she asked. His smile disappeared.

"I was hoping you would buy it", he said.

"Well, I really need to know what I'm buying," she said. "If you know its provenance and if I can verify that you're the rightful owner, I would certainly think about it if the price is reasonable."

"All I want is a thousand dollars," he said, looking at her hopefully.

While that seemed reasonable for such a remarkable quilt, she was wary. "Like I said, Mr..., I'm sorry, I didn't get your name?"

"Gunther, Horace Gunther," he said.

"Well, yes, Mr. Gunther. That seems like a very fair price, but serious quilt buyers always want to know an approximate date, where it came from, and who quilted it. I'm afraid I couldn't get nearly what it's worth without knowing all that."

He started quietly folding the quilt up again. She was sad to see such a beautiful quilt get out of her hands, but maybe it was best. She had an uneasy feeling about the whole situation, so it would be good to get him and the quilt out of the store. "There's an antique dealer in Sparta who specializes in textiles. You should take it to him. He may have a buyer already in mind for something that beautiful. We don't have many requests for quilts, and when we do, they want simple utilitarian quilts, nothing that expensive." She paused for a moment thinking about the woman yesterday looking for appliqued quilts just like this one. "Of course, we did have a woman yesterday looking for a hand-appliqued antique quilt. Maybe I could put you in touch with her. She did say she would come back."

The man's head jerked up. "What did she look like?"

Why on earth would he want to know that, she wondered? Sam interrupted and gave Valerie a look that let him know he really wanted to get the man out of their shop. "Valerie, I don't think this is what she was looking for, was it?"

It *was* what she was looking for and Valerie briefly thought about going ahead and buying the quilt. She could probably double her money, but something just didn't feel right and she had learned to trust her gut feelings. Sam must be feeling the same way. What if the quilt was stolen?

"Mr. Gunther, I think your best bet is to take it to Sparta. Phil Walker is the owner of the store. He knows much more about quilts than I do."

He sighed. It was then that she saw how weary he was. He must have walked quite a ways. Something stirred inside her and instead of feeling repulsed, she felt compassion. "Sir, before you go, may I offer you some refreshment? I have a pot of tea on and some homemade chocolate chip cookies in the back. There's a chaise lounge where you can rest too, if you like. You shouldn't be going back out in this rain with that wheezing cough you have."

Sam gave her a questioning look. She shrugged her shoulders.

"I could use a mite of tea," he said.

"Sam, lead the gentleman to the back room, if you will. The kettle is still plugged in and you know where the tea bags are kept."

"Yes, ma'am," Sam said, with a wink. "I'll give our visitor some refreshments and let him rest. Sir, just follow the sign ahead that says, *Office*." As the man shuffled toward the sign, Sam planted a small kiss on the end of her nose and whispered in her ear. "You're a kind-hearted woman, Valerie Owens." As he walked behind the smelly, unkempt stranger, he smiled thinking about his wife and how she was always putting her faith into action. He had been in such an all-fired hurry to get Mr. Gunther out the door, and here Valerie was feeding him. Valerie had just played out the 45th verse of Matthew 25, *"And he will answer, 'I tell you the truth, when you refused to help the least of these my brothers and sisters, you were refusing to help me'."* He felt ashamed of himself. If it had been up to him, the poor old man would have been booted out the door.

CHAPTER 4

A PLATE OF COOKIES

A good bit later, Sam had forgotten all about having a generous spirit. "That was a mistake," he said pointing his head in a jerking motion to the back room.

Valerie had just finished waiting on their third customer of the day and was tidying up the counter. "Thirty dollars," she said. "At least it was a Christmas item. One less thing to move when we make room for the quilting club." She looked up at Sam. "What was a mistake, dear?"

He sighed. "After two cups of tea and the whole plate of cookies, your new friend took your suggestion and laid back on the lounge chair."

"Oh, that's nice. He must have been famished. Did he rest well?"

"I'll say! He dozed off and thirty minutes later, I had to wake him up because he was snoring so loud, I was afraid it would run off your only customer."

"Poor guy! I could tell he was exhausted." She looked uneasily towards the back. "What's he doing now?"

"Poor guy? Poor me is more like it. I thought I was going to need a crane operator to get him out of that chair, it's so low to the floor. After pulling and tugging and fearing I would pull his arm out of joint, I finally got him up." Sam flexed and turned his back from side to side. "He was deadweight. I'm pretty sure I put my back out trying to lift him."

She smiled to herself. Sam was a darling, but he could be such a big baby at times. She turned him around and started kneading his shoulders, then made her way down to the small of his back.

"Ah, that feels better," he said.

She laughed. "I think the only thing put out, my dear, is you. You're just upset that he ate all the cookies."

He gave her a lopsided smile. "You know me too well. I had already worked up an appetite for cookies dipped in coffee. I poured me a cup after I made his tea, but he held on to that plate for dear life."

Valerie couldn't suppress a smile as she pictured the scene as it played out; Sam eyeing the cookie plate waiting for a chance to swipe one while the messy little man proceeded to wolf them all down. Then a look of concern replaced the smile. "Where is he now?"

"I let him out the back door. It stopped raining."

"I wonder if he has any place to go? He looked…, well, he looked sort of homeless, didn't you think? I hope he stays warm."

"Valerie, I see that look in your eye, and please, don't even think about it. You can't take a stranger in. He may be a serial killer or something. He was warm when he left; his raincoat and rain hat were dry and he had that nice wool scarf around his neck, so he should be fine. If he shows up again and you're still worried about him, I'll take him over to the homeless shelter that the Catholic Church has just started. They haven't had anyone stay overnight yet."

"Where have I been? I didn't know they were doing a homeless shelter."

"I just heard about it last week. It's been in the works ever since that young girl came into town last Christmas and was hiding out in the basement of the Presbyterian church."

"Oh yes, Maria, the one Kit and BJ are trying to adopt."

"Right. I saw Father Thomas in Carter's Drug Store last week. He and Rev Rock from over at the Presbyterian church were talking about it at the lunch counter. All the churches in town are pitching in to help finance the shelter, but St. Gabriel's has the old rectory that's been standing empty for a few years. They've fixed it up and are waiting for their first homeless person."

"I think you should call Father Thomas. Let him know there may be a homeless person in town."

"If you insist," he said. "I'll do it before we lock up."

"That's nice," she said, absentmindedly. She was still wondering what was the story behind their strange visitor. But enough of that! She had things to do if they were going to get her project off the ground. "Sam, go back to the Christmas room and be thinking about where we can put all that stuff."

"March is a hard sell for Christmas items," he said. "People are thinking about Spring and Summer. It's too early to have a Christmas in July sale."

She looked around the room. "Oh, look. We have that nice old rounded display cabinet we got from Cap and Madge's garage sale. That was a good day for us. She practically gave all her nice old things away. Pick out all the things that will display well and start moving them out here. We'll take the rest of it upstairs."

"Not the stairs," he said, rubbing his back again. "The last time I went up there, I sneezed for two solid days. And that fourth step from the top is about to cave in."

"Oh, Sam! I'll take the things to the attic. Or better yet, I'll hire May's grandson to do it. He came in last week to see if we had any part-time work he could do after school. Just do your magic on the display. You have a gift for making things look nice."

He grinned. "I do, don't I?"

She smiled. Her sweet husband was so easily manipulated. He started walking away. She walked over to the Eastlake rocker hoping to get some more research done on her laptop. It wasn't there.

"Sam," she called out to him. "Did you move my computer?"

"Yes, dear. I moved it back in the office. I was afraid you would forget where you put it."

"Who, me?" she said, laughing. She was always laying things down and then having a hard time finding them, especially her cell phone. As she made her way to the office, she thought about all the times she had made Sam call her cell phone number so she could follow the ringtone to find it. Too many; she was certain of that.

When she walked in the office, she noticed Sam had unplugged both the tea kettle and the coffee pot, poured their contents in the sink, cleaned them up and left them to dry on the counter. "What a man!" she said to an empty room, but when she looked closer, she saw he had left the porcelain teapot and matching cups and saucers on the small table in the corner. It was nice of Sam to serve the poor man from one of her better tea services.

One of the cups was turned over on its side and a few drops of tea had spilled over into the saucer. She checked to see if the cup was broken, but it wasn't. The small plate held a half-eaten cookie and some crumbs. It only took her a couple of minutes to tidy it all up. The laptop was just where Sam had put it, on top of the oak writing desk. To get some of the musty odor out of the room, she picked up a can of air freshener and sprayed it all around. She gave the chaise lounge and the worn persian rug under it a liberal spray. That's when she saw it. The bag! She carefully opened it up, wondering what the old man had left behind. She gave a sigh of relief and then one of confusion. The quilt - the beautiful quilt that the man had been so careful and obsessive over. Why had he left it?

"Sam!" Her voice bounced off the walls and Sam came running.

"What's wrong?" he asked.

"Mr. Horace left his bag."

"Who's Mr. Horace?"

"You know! The man with the quilt."

"Well, I'm sure he'll come back for it. He was probably disoriented when I woke him up. I'll bet he'll be back before we close up."

He bet wrong. Dead wrong.

***

Horace Gunther felt he had come to the right place. He had come as far South as his aunt's debit card would bring him. He had paid for a full week in advance at the hotel he was staying in, but when he'd tried withdrawing some money at the ATM inside the hotel this morning, it had rejected the card. Apparently, the lawyer had now closed out the bank accounts as part of the process of liquidating the estate. Now all he had was $100 in the hotel's safe and $35 in his wallet. He had to sell the quilt. He had seen the admiration in the eyes of the owner of the antique shop when he'd shown her the quilt, so he'd left it there on purpose. For one thing, it would be safer there, and if his intuition was right, she would be begging to buy it when he came back tomorrow. All morning, he had a nagging feeling that he was being watched. Trouble was, his poor eyesight made it difficult to spot anyone looking at him with suspicion. Maybe he was just being paranoid. After all, for three days he'd been carrying around a black plastic bag stuffed with a quilt that was worth a fortune to the right collector. Sadly, finding the right collector wasn't going to be easy with a stolen quilt. Stolen? The thought made him furious. It was his quilt; his aunt had told him so. It was in her will, wasn't it? He had watched as she signed the revised will her lawyer had brought to the house just a few months earlier. He had acted as her caregiver for months on end even though it had taken a toll on his own health, with his bad heart. The quilt was to be his reward for all he'd done for her.

He'd gone to the reading of the will just days after his aunt's death, knowing that his cousin was going to be furious when she found Marilee had left the quilt to him. They had both sat in the lawyer's office wide-eyed and stunned when the will had revealed that neither of them had inherited the quilt. His cousin had also been led to believe she was inheriting it. Their aunt had played them both for a fool. Now he was running from two different people who wanted that quilt. The loan shark he'd borrowed money from to bet on the horse races and his cousin, Amelia. Maybe it was paranoia, but he was beginning to think for some reason they were in this thing together. Amelia had been the one who suggested Arlo Balbini as someone he could borrow money from, but after the last few days, he didn't trust either one of them.

He felt a slight quickening in his chest, something he had grown accustomed to, as he stood outside the back entrance of the antique shop he'd just left. He reached in his pocket for his heart medication, but realized he'd left it back at the hotel. It was only a twinge. He spotted a park bench behind one of the other stores in the alley. It was out of the way and no cars were parked anywhere in sight. He would rest for a few minutes on the bench and then go call a cab. At least it had quit raining and the little nap he'd taken in the shop had done him good. As he settled on the bench, he decided it wouldn't hurt to take another little catnap. Besides, he was nice and warm from the hot tea and cookies the nice lady had given him. His clothes were dry and it felt good to sit in the bright sunshine. He was tired, very tired. What tomorrow would bring, he didn't know. With so little money, he knew he had to do something quick.

CHAPTER 5

DEAD WRONG

It was all over town the next morning that a dead body had been found beside the dumpster in the alley behind May's Flower Shop. May herself had discovered it when she carried out the wilted tulips from her flower cooler. She explained to Kathleen Crowder later that morning that she had been walking along with the big box in her arms minding her own business when she saw a man kneeling, almost like he was praying. She called out to him and when he didn't answer, she put the box of spent flowers on the ground and reached to shake his shoulder. At her touch, his body just keeled right over and she screamed bloody murder. Betty had been unlocking the post office door and she ran over to see what the commotion was all about. She joined in the screaming and they both just stood in the alley jumping up and down until a Pepsi-Cola truck driver on his way to make a delivery to Carter's Drug Store heard their racket and stopped. "At least he had the presence of mind to call the police", Kathleen had said. "You two would have been out there all day screaming at each other."

Chief Jess Hamilton recalled that nothing like this had ever happened in Park Place unless you counted the time that Wilbur Hunter had almost got himself killed on the train tracks on the outskirts of town back in 1995. If it hadn't been for Billy Perkins trying to beat the crossarms on Maple Drive, Wilbur would have been squashed as flat as the pennies the boys used to throw on the tracks when the trains came through. He pulled him off the track just in the nick of time. It scared Wilbur straight. He never took another drink of liquor and died sober at the ripe old age of eighty-eight.

The death of the man in the alley was obviously foul play since there were signs of a struggle and there were strangulation marks around the man's neck. The only identification was a veteran's ID card in a worn-out billfold. The picture on the card matched the body, and the man's name was Horace Gunther. Jess walked from shop to shop on Main Street interviewing all the merchants. Junie Crowder from the Feed and Seed Store had already popped in the back door of The Banty Hen and told Sam and Valerie about the body. Sam was fretting and wringing his hands when Jess walked in.

"He came in here yesterday," Sam said. "If only I had asked him a few more questions and taken the time to walk him down to the Catholic church, he might be alive now! I should have listened to Valerie."

"Catholic church? Did he want to see a priest?" Jess asked.

"No, nothing like that. Valerie said he looked like a homeless man and I should have made sure he got some help."

Valerie was right beside him. "Calm down, Sam. It was just an observation, and you did call Father Thomas about him before we left the shop."

"Only because you insisted, Valerie. I was just going to forget about him. He made me uncomfortable. I should have called you, Jess."

"Stop beating up on yourself, Sam. We didn't really know if he was homeless. Besides, we both thought he would come back to pick up the quilt."

"The quilt?" Jess was confused. "What's this about a quilt?"

"There it is," Sam said, pointing to the bag. "He came in here trying to sell us this quilt for a thousand dollars..."

Valerie interrupted. "But without knowing the provenance of the quilt, we couldn't pay that much...."

Jess was getting more confused by the minute. "Hold up. Let me get this straight. You saw this man just yesterday and he came in here trying to sell you an expensive quilt but you didn't buy it; is that right?"

"Yes, that's what happened."

"Well, why do you still have the quilt?"

Sam stuttered. "Well, he drank two cups of tea and ate a whole plate of chocolate chip cookies and took a nap and..."

Valerie broke in. "And Sam woke him up because he was snoring and I had a customer in the store who bought a measly thirty-dollar Christmas item and it was only our third customer of the day."

"And I hurt my back trying to get him out of the lounge chair and..."

Jess laughed. "I can see you're both pretty worked up. Let's sit down and get this straightened out." He looked around. "Do you have any more of those cookies?"

Sam looked downcast and whined. "No, he ate them all."

"But I made some peanut butter cookies last night," Valerie chimed in. "Come on back to the office and I'll pour us all a cup of coffee. I sure need one."

Jess smiled. "I think it's going to take more than a cup of coffee and a cookie to straighten this out."

Sam finally seemed to realize how confusing it had all sounded, and laughed. "Just so you don't eat the whole plate."

"Sam!" Valerie looked crushed. "Please don't bring that up! You've been complaining about the poor man eating the whole plate of cookies, when it was probably the last thing he had to eat." She got a tissue from the box on the counter and held it to her nose, sniffing into it. "And we weren't very nice to him." She blew her nose and looked up at Sam. "But at least his last meal was served on fine china."

Sam put his arm around his wife. "Valerie honey, I'm sorry. You offered him food and drink and a place to rest. You brought him a little bit of happiness on a dreary day. I was the one complaining."

Jess shook his head, and wondered if he would ever get anything coherent out of those two.

***

A pot of coffee and a half plate of cookies later, Jess was trying to wrap up his interview with the Owenses. "What was he wearing when he came inside the shop?"

"When he came in he had on a raincoat, a slicker to be exact, you know, one of those yellow things with a matching hat. It was dripping wet when he came in."

"But it was nice and dry when he left," Sam said. "And don't forget the wool scarf. It was brown, wasn't it, Valerie?"

"Yes, a deep, rich brown, and it looked much nicer than the clothes he wore under the raincoat. They were all wrinkled up and looked as if he'd worn them for days."

"He wore a scarf?" Jess asked. "He didn't have on a scarf when he was found."

"Yes, I distinctly remember he had on the scarf when he left. He even mentioned how much better he felt since he was nice and dry."

Valerie let out a long breath. "Sam, are you sure? You're not very observant at times. You didn't even notice that he left without his bag."

"Valerie, I've never been more sure of anything! He had on that scarf when he walked out the door. As a matter of fact, he never took it off, even while he was napping."

"Don't get so worked up, dear. I believe you. I'm just shaken up a little."

"That's understandable," Jess said. "We'll look again. The murderer must have removed it because he couldn't very well get a choke-hold on him with a scarf on."

"Oh no, is that how the poor man died? That's so cruel!" Valerie was almost in tears. Jess changed the subject.

"You haven't seen any other suspicious people come in, have you?"

"I'm trying to remember," Valerie said. "We have quite a few out-of-towners stop in from the big sign we have out on the interstate. They love our quaint little Main Street and I think the sign helps some of the other merchants in town too. Especially the candy shop and the lunch counter at Carter's. And we always tell them about BJ's Diner for some good Southern food."

"Has there been anyone recently? Maybe someone asking about old quilts?"

"We had someone on Monday from Sun's Up, but she was just asking if there was a quilting group in town that she could join. She's been in before - a regular customer, and she gave me her phone number so I'm sure she's above board. Her name is Kay." She reached around and plucked a card from her desk. "Here it is, Kay Bishop."

"What about the tall woman with a Northern accent who came in here Monday, Valerie? She was asking if we had any antique quilts, wasn't she?"

"Yes, I was going to mention her next. She was in here the same time as Kay. She was a little snooty, wasn't she, Sam? And rather ditzy, I might add. I couldn't make her understand I didn't have any antique quilts!"

"Yeah," he said, laughing. "You dubbed her the Queen of Sheba when you told me about her."

"Had you ever seen her before?"

Valerie thought a moment before answering. "No, I don't think so."

"But you're not sure?"

"No, I was just thinking about something else. I'm sure I haven't seen her before, but she did have one outstanding feature that I noticed. It was a red heart-shaped birthmark on her left cheek near her hairline."

Jess didn't say anything. The coroner said Horace Gunther had a heart-shaped birthmark on his right shoulder. Coincidence? Did birthmarks run in families?

"Call me if she comes back in. I'm sure it's nothing, but since she was asking about old quilts, it could be a lead. We have nothing else to go on. I'll have to take the quilt back to the police station. It's now considered evidence."

"Please do," Valerie said. "It would be a constant reminder if it stayed here. Besides, we don't know who it belongs to with Mr. Horace dead."

"I think finding out the quilt's ownership will be a key to solving the murder," Jess said. "We'll start by trying to find the man's next-of-kin. And I need to ask you not to let anyone know that he left the quilt with you."

"Of course," Sam said, "but we seem to be the last ones who saw him alive. If the murder has something to do with the quilt, and someone was watching him, wouldn't they assume the quilt was here when they didn't find it on him?"

"It's very possible," Jess said. "Keep your back door locked and call me if you have any trouble." He gave Valerie his card. "This is my direct cell phone number. I always answer it immediately and the station is only two blocks away."

"Just long enough for someone to knock me over the head!" Sam said.

"Sam! You're scaring me!"

"I'm just teasing, Valerie," he said, trying to reassure her, but he did feel a little uneasy. As Jess walked out the door carrying the bag, Sam waved goodbye. "Adios and good riddance, quilt. You've caused us nothing but trouble."

CHAPTER 6

A STITCH IN TIME

When Jess got back to the station, he put the bag on the receptionist's desk. "Heather, when Cliff comes in, ask him if he'll do some research on quilts like this one. The man who was murdered last night left this bag at the antique store by mistake. It may have something to do with the murder."

"Wow," Heather said, "who would kill someone over a quilt?"

"It's apparently an expensive quilt. When a person is carrying around something valuable and someone else wants it.... Well, it's all about greediness, I suppose. People have been killed over a handful of dollar bills in the victim's pockets. And remember, just less than two years ago, how the greedy real estate agent over in Sparta tried to poison Rev Rock because he was interfering with the big buy-up of riverfront property she was trying to make?"

"How could I forget that one?" she said. "His poor cat ended up poisoned instead. By the way, the phone has been ringing off the hook this morning. People are scared because there's a killer on the loose."

"I don't think they need to be worried. The only ones I'm concerned about are the Owenses. They were the last ones to see Mr. Gunther alive. Ask Cliff to double up his Main Street drive-bys. Tell him to check the alley at least twice a day too."

"Okay, I will. Did the old man have any other valuables on him? Maybe it was someone trying to rob him of his money and he fought back and they killed him."

"Believe me, Horace Gunther was in no shape to fight back. And his wallet didn't appear to be taken out of his pocket before he died. He only had $35 and a debit card, but a robber usually takes the victim's wallet. I don't think they would take the time to put it back in his pocket after they killed him."

"That's true." She turned to walk away. "I'll get on my computer and try to research the quilt for you."

"Thanks Heather. I'll be in my office making some phone calls. I need to find a next-of-kin for our dead man." He started to walk away but doubled back. "Heather, would you mind calling Father Thomas at St. Gabriel's and ask him if I can come by later today. I need to talk to him about the homeless shelter. On second thought, ask if he can meet me at the diner at around 1:15."

"Sure thing."

***

Jess sat at his desk with the folder he'd made for Horace Gunther opened in front of him. How on earth did the man end up in Park Place, of all places. Small towns rarely had to deal with murders.

Being a small-town cop was all Jess had ever wanted to be. His father was Vice-President of Putnam Mills, a large textile mill in the lower part of the state where he and his brother and sister grew up. The other two had gone to Clemson University, but Jess had only wanted to go to the local community college and get a two-year degree in Police Science. His father had been disappointed and accused him of having no ambition, but he got his degree and landed a job on the police force in Columbia. He met Rebecca at a single's party at church and it wasn't long before he proposed. Her bachelor's degree was in social work and one day as she was combing the classified section of The State Newspaper, she came upon an employment ad that looked promising in a small town in the upper part of the state. Right below it was another ad, one that she knew Jess would be interested in. When their interviews went well and they were hired, they knew it was part of God's plan. Park Place had just incorporated into a township and despite his lack of experience, they hired Jess as their Police Chief. At the same time, Beverly Hills Children's Home just outside the town limits was hiring a live-in house parent. Rebecca's degree in Behavioral Science overqualified her, but they hired her anyway. Jess rented a bedroom in the home of an older couple on Commerce Street, just a block from the police station. It wasn't long before the director of the Children's Home retired and Rebecca slid right into the job. It was also required that the director live on campus, and a suite of rooms was set aside on the first floor for her. After she settled in, she and Jess got married and he moved into the old mansion with her. They had been in Park Place going on twenty years, and although they were never able to have children of their own, they nurtured and loved all the children that came through the doors of the home. Some stayed only a few nights, others were there for months, and several had been placed there as young children and aged out at eighteen. Those were the ones who captured their hearts.

Jess closed the folder and opened his desk drawer, dropping it inside. It had taken just one phone call to find where Horace had lived before he ended up in his present circumstances in cold storage at Griffin's Funeral Home. His veteran's ID card didn't list an address but when Jess called the Veteran's Administration in Washington, DC, they pulled up almost everything by reading the barcode that ran down the right-hand side of the card. They gave his address as Aberdeen, Maryland. With a little further investigation, it was found that he didn't have a valid driver's license because he couldn't pass the eye exam, and a quick background check showed that he had never been in trouble with the law except for a domestic dispute in Annapolis that ended up with the charges being dropped. He also learned that his apartment complex in Aberdeen was government low-income housing. When Horace filled out a rental form, he had listed two next-of-kin; an aunt who had recently passed away and a first cousin, Amelia Reinhart, who lived in Annapolis. Hmm…, could he and the cousin be at each other's throats? If so, it appeared this Amelia had gotten the upper hand. Pure speculation, he reminded himself, but it paid to leave no stone unturned. He had made two attempts to call her, but there was no answer. He left a message on her answering machine. If he couldn't reach her by the end of the day, he would call the police precinct in her area and have them inform her of her cousin's death.

Deputy Cliff Jordan first knocked and then stuck his head in the door. "May I come in?"

"Come on in. You must have some information for me."

"Heather does. She said you wanted to see me. She's got some information about the quilt."

"Have her come in too."

Cliff stepped back and motioned to Heather to go in ahead of him. "She's been busy on the computer. She wanted me to relay it to you, but she can tell you herself much better than I can pass it along. I might lose something in the re-telling."

Jess laughed. "Probably so, especially since you don't know anymore about quilts than I do." He stood up while Heather walked in with the bag in one hand and some papers in the other. "Just leave the door open, Cliff, since we don't have anyone manning the desk out there." He pointed to the two chairs in front of his desk. "Y'all have a seat."

"I'll stand for now," Heather said. "I think you need a visual for this one." She took the quilt out of the bag as Cliff sat down. "I'll just spread it out here." She unfolded it and laid it lengthwise across the chair.

"Wow," Cliff said. "You're right about me not knowing anything about quilts, but that one sure is pretty." Jess nodded in agreement.

"It's called a Baltimore Album Quilt," Heather said. "You see, each block is hand appliquéd, then they're sewn together and quilted. Each quilt has its own unique design. I doubt that you could ever find two just alike unless they were quilted by the same person, and even then, there would be some variation. Some have appliquéd blocks of old monuments or buildings, some are in starburst designs, and some, like this one are made with a floral theme." She pointed to one particular block of the quilt. "From what I've read, this flower basket design was one of the most tedious to make." She ran her hand over the small stitches. "But back to the name. When you look at it...." She started folding it from the top, keeping the fold along the lines of where the blocks were stitched together. Then she unfolded it one line of blocks at a time. "See!"

"Aha," Jess said. "I guess that's why it's called an album quilt. It's almost like looking at a picture album."

"Right! And in that day, most young women of any social status had hard cover albums where they collected autographs, popular sayings, postcards, tradecards and other colorful paper or fabric designs. Some researchers think these albums were the inspiration for the quilt designs. There were several particularly talented women who made the designs and this quilt has the signature of one of these women. See right here, in the middle block it has her signature, Mary Evans. And they aren't true Baltimore quilts unless they were made in Baltimore. So far, I've been checking the designs, when they were made, and the prices they bring."

"Do you think this one is worth what Horace was asking for it?"

"How much was that?"

"A thousand dollars."

Cliff's mouth flew open. "Who-wee! That seems like an awful lot for a quilt."

"So far, I haven't found any with a selling price for under $10,000, and that one was crudely made. The time-period was the 1840's through about 1865, and apparently, they're hard to find in this condition and they weren't made in great numbers. One reason is they were time-consuming, plus the ladies who made them weren't just common quilters. They had to be talented in both quilting and embroidery and most were well-to-do women. Women without means were too busy trying to feed their families and the quilts they made were for keeping warm on cold winter nights." She held up the quilt and pointed to one of the blocks. "Just look at that," she said. Look at all the tiny little stitches in this one block. Examples much like this one have sold at auction houses to museums and collectors for anywhere between thirty and forty thousand dollars, and quilts by this particular designer have sold for over $100,000."

Jess shook his head. "And to think Mr. Gunther was carrying it around in that old plastic bag - in the rain, even."

Heather sighed. "And the poor man was murdered because of it." She looked like she might cry any minute. "I'm sure this quilt started out in loving hands. What a sad ending." She started folding it up. "I think this beauty is deserving of a new bag, don't you?"

"Yes, and maybe a bank vault." He watched as she folded it. "Seriously, as soon as you get it stored in a clean bag, I'll take it downstairs to the evidence room and lock it in the cage that only you and I have the key to. That way, I'll be responsible for its security."

Heather draped it over her arm and carried it to a small table in the corner of Jess's office. Before she put it down, she patted it with her hand. "Poor little quilt," she said. "Maybe someday soon you can come out of that cold dark basement and be displayed in a museum where something as pretty as you should be."

Jess and Cliff exchanged glances and smiled as she laid it down. "It may be a while, Heather. First, we have to find Mr. Gunther's next-of-kin. Unless specified in the will, they'll inherit it. You've done great on the research."

"I'll keep looking", she said. "Maybe there's a registry somewhere of known owners."

"Good idea." He turned to his deputy. "Cliff, I want you to patrol Main Street heavily until we find the murderer."

"You mean if we find the murderer. He's probably long gone by now," Cliff said.

"I don't think so. There were no witnesses. We have a valuable quilt which may or may not be the motive behind the murder. No one knows about the quilt except the three of us and Sam and Valerie. I've already told them to keep that information under wraps and I'm asking you to do the same." They both nodded. "Valerie and Sam may be in trouble if the murderer was following the victim and knows he went into the shop with the quilt and came out without it."

"I'll keep my eye on the shop. Do you want me to do it undercover?"

"Yes, otherwise he'll stay away and we may never find him. Now, we've got a lot to do, but first, let's eat these donuts someone brought by."

Heather giggled. "That was Rev Rock. He heard about the murder and thought you might need something to give you energy."

"That was nice of him, but I've already had some peanut butter cookies at The Banty Hen," Jess said as he opened the box. "Hooray! Two lemon-filled; you guys can have the rest." He got a paper plate from his desk drawer and put the two donuts on it. "This will be my lunch."

"I've got dibs on the chocolate," Heather said.

"So, that means I get to eat the other eight," Cliff said, grabbing the box.

"You wish," Heather said. "Carrie will have your hide if you eat eight donuts. She's already got you on a diet."

Cliff blushed. "How do you know?"

"I've been seeing those little portion containers in the fridge with salads and fruits. If you'll give me five bucks, I won't tell her you've been seen hanging around BJ's Diner with the lunch crowd."

"That's extortion," Cliff said. "It's against the law. Can I arrest her, Jess?"

Jess laughed. "Get to work you two." Then he grew serious. "Looks like we've got a murderer in Park Place to capture."

CHAPTER 7

MISS, MRS. AND MS

Just as he expected, the rumors about the murder of Horace Gunther were running rampant. When Jess stopped by the post office to mail some invitations to an open house event at the orphanage, he thought Betty was going to jump over the counter to get the latest developments in the case. "It's my job as postmistress to keep people informed," she said. "You do know this is the hub of the town, don't you?"

"I'm well aware of that, Betty. And you can be sure that you'll be one of the first people to find out when we're ready to make public any progress we're making. But right now, I don't have anything to report."

"Hmph!" she said. "Well, be that way, but unless I know, I can't stop all the rumors floating around."

"What kind of rumors?" he asked.

"I don't know. Just all kinds of things."

"If you've heard anything, I need to know. Even the smallest detail can be a clue." he said, trying to make his voice sound tough and official. "Otherwise if you've heard something and are not telling it, you could be charged with obstruction of justice."

Betty's eyes got wide, then the sassy expression he was accustomed to took over and she put her hands on her hips. "Don't you be threatening me with no old obstruction of justice or whatever you said, Jess Hamilton. You know I was just fishing for information. How else am

I going to keep my status of best-news-source-in-town if you don't tell me anything!"

He laughed. "Betty, you know I'll tell you when I can. In the meanwhile, keep your ears open and report to me if you hear anything. Someone walking along Main Street may have seen or heard something important that day and didn't think it had anything to do with the murder."

Betty perked up. "Yeah, it would be something if I solved the case for you." She looked out from over the frames of her reading glasses and gave him a smirky look. "Then the people in town will elect me the police chief next year."

"I'm sorry to disappoint you, Betty, but I'm not an elected official. I'm hired by the Town of Park Place."

"Aha," she said, the smirk still in place. "But I know the mayor!"

It was just as bad when he walked in the diner. Walt Harrington, who was hard of hearing, called him over to his table. Not being able to hear, he seemed to think no one else could either because he talked loud enough to be heard out in the parking lot. "I heard we've got a serial killer on the loose, Jess. What are you doing about it?"

"Walt, I'm afraid you heard wrong. As far as we know, there's only been one victim in town, and we're working on it as fast as we can."

"Well, you better catch him quick before he kills again," Walt said.

"We'll do our best," he shouted back at Walt, realizing the older man hadn't heard a word he'd said. He saw Father Thomas at a booth near the back and made his way to where he sat.

"I'll bet it was one of those construction people working on the Catawba River bridge," Burt Mason said as Jess walked by. BJ, the owner of the diner was refilling iced tea glasses at another table and overheard.

"Listen Burt, we haven't had a minute's trouble out of any of those construction workers. As a matter of fact, we have the diner about full of them today." He pointed around the room. Several tough looking men were glaring at Burt, and he blushed. He got up quickly and left a half-finished hamburger on his plate.

"I've got to get back to work now," he told BJ. "I'll leave a ten-spot at the register. That ought to cover the meal and my tip." BJ nodded, and Burt rushed out the door.

"People can't help speculating," BJ said, as he stood there a minute talking to Jess. "But I don't want them spreading rumors about my customers. There are a lot of good men in that bridge crew and the diner and other businesses in town have sure benefited from having them here." He looked at Jess. "Are you here by yourself or are you meeting someone?"

"I'm meeting Father Thomas back there," he said, pointing to the booth where the priest was sitting.

"Need a menu?"

"No, I'm just having coffee today, thank you."

"I'll bring it right over. That's what Father Thomas is having too." Go ahead and sit down. I'm shorthanded on staff today, so I'll bring your coffee."

Jess laughed. "I'll be sure to leave a tip."

The priest stood when Jess got to the booth and they shook hands. By the time BJ brought their coffee, they had already started their conversation.

"All we have to go by is the picture on his veteran ID card," Jess said. "But it looks like he's carried it in his wallet for years. It looks like him but I would like to get a positive identification." He put a healthy shot of cream in his coffee and stirred it as he waited for a comment from Father Thomas. He looked up. The priest was adding sugar to his cup.

"I've tried my best to give up sugar," he said. My waist and my pre-diabetes diagnosis have given me every reason to, but that old devil that sits on my shoulder, tells me I must have it."

Jess laughed. "I've always thought you Catholics avoided talking about the devil," he said. "You're supposed to leave that up to us Protestants."

"I guess we think if we don't talk about him, he'll leave us alone." His eyes were twinkling. "Now back to your situation. What happens now? How will you get a positive ID?"

"We've sent the photo to the police department in his hometown, and one to Annapolis where his cousin lives. They'll go by his apartment complex and see if someone can identify him. At the same time, the Annapolis police will take it to his cousin's home. I've tried all day to reach her, so now I'm waiting for them to call back."

"Have you tried Facebook?" Father Thomas asked. "Apparently, you can reach everyone anywhere on Facebook these days, or so I've been told by my younger parishioners. They keep urging me to get a Facebook page."

Jess laughed. He liked this priest. Father Thomas had been assigned to St. Gabriel's Parish when their old priest retired just a few months earlier. This was the first time he'd had a chance to talk with him other than speaking when they passed.

"Well, no. That's one place I haven't tried."

"You asked to see me, Jess. Is there something I can do to help?"

"Sam told me he called you yesterday about the murder victim. Valerie was worried that he had no place to go."

"I've thought about that all morning. I did talk to Sam and told him if the man showed up again, to call me. My assistant was in the office when I got the call and offered to go check on him, but I didn't think it was necessary. Now I've been beating myself up thinking if one of us had just gone over there and looked for him, this never would have happened and he could have had a warm, dry place to stay overnight instead of ending up dead in a dark alley. Poor man!"

"You didn't exactly have a crystal ball. No one could have known this would happen. For all we knew, he could have been staying at one of the hotels off the interstate. I've faxed a photo to each of them, and I'm waiting to hear back after all the different front desk staff get a chance to look at it. The day shift didn't recognize the man at all, but the night shift hasn't come in yet. None of them had a Horace Gunther registered, so if he's staying somewhere close, he's doing it under a fake name."

"What about transportation? Did he have his own car?"

"No, he doesn't even have a driver's license. I've called all the taxi companies for miles around and he didn't use any of their services. Of course, if he is staying nearby, he could have walked or hitchhiked. He's a heavy man though, and doesn't look like a walker, but Valerie did say he appeared to be exhausted and rain-soaked, so it's possible he was on foot."

"Maybe he has relatives in town."

"It's possible. There were only two relatives listed on his rental agreement, but one was an elderly aunt who has died in the meanwhile. But that doesn't mean anything. You're only required to list your next-of-kin, so he could have fifty relatives for all we know. If he's staying with someone around here, I hope they'll hear it on the news and come forward to claim his body. They should be missing him by now."

Jess finished off his coffee and immediately the red-headed waitress came to fill it up. It was Kit Jones, BJ's wife, the perky fireball half of BJ's Diner."

"Boys, we're going to be closing here in about twenty minutes. Ya' sure I can't get you something to eat? Jess, I've never seen you come in here without ordering BJ's famous banana pudding."

"Not today, Kit. I would probably die from a sugar overdose. I've already had five of Valerie's peanut butter cookies and two lemon-filled donuts today." He turned to his guest at the table. "How about you, Father? I'm paying."

"Banana Pudding is one of my weaknesses, Mrs. Jones, but until I get my blood sugar under control, I'm afraid I'll have to pass. It might put me in a diabetic coma."

"Well Father, I just might put you in some kind of coma if you keep calling me Mrs. Jones. Every time you do, I look over my shoulder to see if BJ's mama has come back from the dead. My name is Kit, and with all due respect to your priesthood, I beg you to call me that."

Jess laughed out loud as Father Thomas turned a deep shade of red, but then he recovered and his eyes once again twinkled.

"Well then young lady, I insist you call me Thomas."

Kit's eyes got wide as saucers. "You know I can't do that, Father."

He smiled. "See, it would be the same with me, Mrs. Jones. I can no more call you Kit than you can call me Thomas. I guess I'm what most people call old-school. I learned from an old priest that I should never call a lady by her first name. He said that it implies intimacy and we should simply call women Miss, Ms, or Mrs., whichever applies. It's much more respectful."

Kit put the coffee pot on the table and reached out to shake his hand. She gave it a firm clasp which almost made him wince. "Touche, Father, it's not everyday that Kit Jones gets her comeuppance, but you did it without even ruffling my feathers. I like you, Father Thomas, I really do, and if you want to call me Mrs. Jones, that's fine with me."

He smiled, seemingly pleased with himself. Kit let go of his hand and leaned over the table. "But if you ever want to be intimate enough to call me by my first name, please let me know," she said. "I'm pretty sure it wouldn't require much more than a handshake." She stood up straight. She picked up the coffee pot and sashayed off to another table as Father Thomas blushed again, and the chief of police spewed out the coffee he had just sipped from his cup.

Father Thomas recovered from the shock. "If I could hide under this table, I would," he said.

"And if I knew I could get back up, I would roll on the floor laughing," Jess said when he finally caught his breath. "For a minute there, I thought you had her, but I should have known better. Nobody gets one up on Kit Jones."

CHAPTER 8

AN OPEN DOOR

The sun was shining brightly through the old oak trees on Church Street as the members of Park Place Presbyterian walked through the parking lot and up the steps of the Gothic Revival style brick church with the belltower. Clarence Foster had arrived early to get a good parking space and had been sitting in the car watching the play of shadows the sun was making in the trees adjoining the church property. The filtering effect of the sun intensified the bright green of the young leaves that were blowing in the warm breeze. A wave of sadness washed over him and he wished Teresa was sitting beside him to enjoy the change of seasons here in the Carolinas that she had loved so much. He and Teresa had bought a house in the up and growing panhandle of Lancaster County when he retired from the police force in Jacksonville, Florida not quite two years earlier. She had always lived in Florida where most of the trees and shrubbery stayed green year-round. He remembered their first winter and how thrilled she had been to see a major snowfall in January. No matter that it was here today and gone tomorrow, she loved it just the same. Then when the stark empty branches of winter turned into a sea of green in late March, she was equally thrilled. They had both looked forward to his retirement; she more than he, because she was always worried for his safety, so when she was diagnosed with an incurable cancer, he surprised her by quitting the force and making the move to South

Carolina, bringing them closer to their grandchildren to live out her remaining days.

Now she was gone. Just eight months after their move, she died and he was left bereft and alone in the big house they had built. He loved the change of seasons too, but now that he was trying to move on with his life, he had small tinges of regret that he had retired so early. He had been fifty years old at the time with twenty-eight years on the force. Now he was closing in on fifty-two and was ready to go back to work, at least part-time. He was bored.

He was startled out of his reminiscing by a knock on the passenger side window. It was Vic Battles, the neighbor who first suggested that he and Teresa try Park Place Presbyterian. They both fell in love with it and had planned to join right before she passed away. He opened the door and got out. Vic and Nancy waited for him to walk in with them.

"I see you're late too," Nancy said. "At least they haven't rung the bells yet." Just as soon as the words came out of her mouth, the tall belltower above them belched out the first chime. "I spoke too early," she said, and they all rushed to the front door.

Rev Rock sat in the seat behind the pulpit and looked out at the congregation as the liturgist read the announcements. The membership was growing and there were very few empty seats, which was a good thing. Five people had joined just in the last month, the latest was Clarence Foster, sitting on the second row from the front. He'd had a good conversation with Clarence and his wife Teresa when they expressed an interest in joining, but when Teresa passed away not long after they spoke, Clarence put it off until recently. He had been so touched by the amount of love and support Park Place Presbyterian gave him after his loss and said there was no other church in the world he'd rather be a part of. Now that Teresa was gone, he sensed that Clarence was itching to find something productive to do. He would talk to him about some of the mission projects the church was doing and see if any of them would be a good fit for him.

Before Rock knew it, the liturgist had finished the readings, the first hymn was being sung, and it was time for him to get behind the pulpit to give his sermon titled, *An Open Door.*

"One of the scripture readings this morning comes from Acts 12:1-17 and the other from Acts 16:6-10." He read both readings and as he was delivering the sermon, everyone was attentive, especially Clarence.

Clarence was paying rapt attention and as Rock was wrapping it all up, he felt the last part was geared just for him. He listened as Rock continued.

"I'm sure that all of you have heard the expression, *When God closes one door, He opens another.* This expression doesn't come from scripture, but I've found it to be true in many ways. Our lives can change in a flash with the shutting and opening of doors. In Acts 12, Peter was being held in prison and would be put to death the next day. And what happened? God sent an angel and opened the doors for him. The prison doors opened, the city gates opened, but when he reached the house where people were praying for him, the door was closed. These doors literally changed Paul's life."

"Then in *Acts 16:6-10*, As Paul and Timothy traveled to Macedonia, Paul found and experienced two closed doors. Because those doors were closed, he was led to God's plan for him, an open door of ministry. Just look at how these doors changed the course of history!"

"Have you experienced closed doors on your path recently? Have you looked to Him to lead you to open doors?"

On his way out, Clarence stopped and shook hands with Rock. "You were preaching to me, today, Rev Rock."

"The scripture does seem to call our names sometimes, doesn't it?"

Clarence nodded. "It had my name written all over it. With all that's happened recently, I've been wrestling with the fact that too many doors in my life have been closing, and after listening to you today, I'm wondering if God is getting ready to open up another door."

"You never know," Rock said. "He works best when we learn to be patient and don't rush things."

"But I want it now," Clarence said, laughing.

Rock laughed with him. "Be careful what you wish for," he said. "He may drop something demanding on your plate and when He does, you'll need to remember another scripture passage. *I can do all things through Christ who strengthens me. Philippians 4:13.*"

CHAPTER 9

THE SOUND OF MUSIC

Two days had passed without any new information, and then Jess got a phone call. The Queen's Inn had been rather grand in her heyday, but poor management had damaged her reputation and she was no longer living up to her name. The inn had become one of the less desirable places to stay along the interstate outside of town. The night clerk had heard about the murder on TV and knew that one of their guests fit the description. She remembered registering Horace Gunther almost a week before under the alias of John Bayley which Jess found interesting since Bayley was the last name of the recently deceased aunt. But apparently, there was a reason he used the Bayley last name. He had used Marilee Bayley's debit card, the one found in his wallet. No one had seen him come and go from the motel, but that wasn't unusual since his room was on the first floor near a side entrance that he could unlock with his key-card. The maid had noticed that his bed hadn't been slept in for the last three nights, but sometimes their guests just up and left without telling them.

Jess, Cliff and Heather were once again meeting in his office. "I thought it was time for a fact gathering session again," he said. "Cliff, you first. Have you seen any unusual activity around the antique store or the alley behind it?"

"There's been no one in the alley except our own locals wanting to see where the murder happened.

Everyone who has come through The Banty Hens' doors are local people too, except for a tall skinny man looking for antique fishing lures, two ladies registering for the new quilting class Valerie is organizing, and a nun."

"Those classes must be popular. Rebecca said last night that she has registered. Was the tall skinny man someone they knew?"

"No, he told Sam he'd seen the sign advertising the antique store out on the interstate. He was just passing through."

"Was the nun just passing through, too?"

"No, she's here in town at St. Gabriels."

"That's funny, I just talked to Father Thomas a few days ago and he didn't mention a nun."

"I went over to the church to check it out. She was outside the old rectory. Did you know they've fixed it up for a homeless shelter?" Jess nodded. "She was sweeping off the steps. A bunch of leaves and twigs had blown in with the storm last week. I stopped and talked with her a minute. She said she'd been sent by the diocese to assist with the homeless shelter."

"Oh," Jess said, "maybe that's who Father Thomas was referring to when he was talking about an assistant."

"She seemed nice enough and she was attractive in a different sort of way."

"Different? How so?"

He paused a moment. "I don't know. I guess I've just never considered that nuns should be pretty, but she certainly is."

"How old is she?"

"I'm a terrible judge of ages, but I would say mid-to-late thirties. She said they haven't had any overnight guests in the shelter yet, but they've fed a few people."

"Those nuns are amazing," Heather said, "but I could never be one."

"Why's that," Jess asked.

"I guess I'm too boy-crazy," she said with a grin.

"Yeah, and all the nuns I've seen on TV are either old or plain looking," Cliff said.

Jess knew they were getting off track, but he couldn't help but join in. "I don't know," he said. "Julie Andrews was pretty in *The Sound of Music.*"

"Who's Julie Andrews?" Heather asked.

"What's *the Sound of Music?*" Cliff asked.

Jess shook his head. "Never mind. I'm just showing my age. Heather, did you find out any more about those quilts? Anything that might be important to the case?"

"The Baltimore Museum of Art does have a registry with all known owners, but it's confidential. I asked for it as a law enforcement request, but the administrator of their website told me we would have to have a court order to look at it."

"We won't bother with that for the time being," Jess said. "But if we hit a complete dead end, we'll look at it further." He shuffled the papers on his desk, put them back in the file folder and stood up. "I think that about wraps it up for now. I'm going to finish this paperwork, then get out of here for a while. It's a shame we have to be suspicious of everyone new in town, but we can't overlook any possibilities."

He didn't tell them about the phone calls he'd received earlier in the day. The police in Aberdeen had gone inside Mr. Gunther's apartment and found it ransacked. The same with his cousin's home in Annapolis. The people in her workplace had asked for a wellness check because she failed to report back to work after asking for a few days off. Her house had been broken into and was a mess, with drawers turned upside down, closets emptied and her bed sheets pulled off and scattered on the floor. They were treating her case as a missing person's report with foul play suspected, especially now that her cousin had turned up dead. The only productive information so far was that cousin Amelia's only next-of-kin were the same dead aunt and the now dead Horace. If she was dead too, it would be the end of the family tree. The Annapolis police were interviewing the missing woman's neighbors to determine if they had seen anyone suspicious hanging around.

Jess drummed his fingers on the table. Sometimes he wished he had hired a more seasoned officer than Cliff. He was young and had only been on the force for three years. The town had such a small budget, they couldn't afford to pay anyone higher up on the pay scale. Of course, he'd never had a murder case in Park Place before, so there hadn't been much need for an experienced ear to be a sounding board until now. He did have the county's sheriff he could call on but he had such a heavy load to carry already. He pulled his Rolodex out and started thumbing through his contacts. He quit scrolling when he came upon one entry. It was the cell phone number of the pastor of Park Place Presbyterian Church, his own pastor, Rock Clark. Maybe a little spiritual guidance would help. He dialed the number.

"Sure, come on over," Rock said. "I was going to the hospital to see Clay Harper, but his wife just called to say they released him this afternoon and he's too exhausted for me to come for a visit."

Jess got up and walked out of his office and into the reception area. "Heather, I'll be over at the church office if you need me," he said.

"Sure," she said. "Tell Miss Reva I said hello, and oh, wait just a second." She pulled something out from under the desk. Would you mind taking this casserole dish to her. She made Momma a chicken casserole last week when she was sick. There's a thank you note attached. I told her I would drive it over, but since you're going anyway...."

***

Reva, the church secretary had her customary plate of brownies sitting on the coffee table when Jess walked in. He wondered how Rev Rock stayed so thin with all the sweets Reva made. Of course, he had noticed that since Rock got married, he'd put on a little weight. He'd been a bachelor so long, and now that Liz and Reva were both cooking for him, he didn't stand a chance.

He handed Reva the casserole dish. "Just go on in, Jess," she said. "He's waiting for you."

Rock pointed to one of the empty chairs when he walked into the room. "Sit a spell," he said. "I'm glad you came. I needed a break."

"I don't know what I need," Jess said. "This case has got me stumped and I don't have anyone to hash it out with."

"Detective work is a little out of my league," Rock said. "But I'm a good listener."

"Hmm.... That is complicated," Rock said when Jess finished talking. "Could they have ransacked each other's houses looking for the quilt? Maybe one of them stole it from the other, and the other tried to get it back."

"I had thought of that," Jess said. "But with the cousin missing, we don't have much to go on."

"I meant to call you the morning after the murder about something Liz saw, but I got sidetracked. It was probably nothing, though."

"Nothing's too small when it comes to observations," Jess said. "What was it?"

"During the big storm on Monday, Liz was at the post office. She and the others saw a lone figure walking to the dumpster not far from where the body was found, but they all thought it was one of the other merchants on Main Street. Liz said it reminded her of the apparition of a grim reaper, tall and thin, hunched over with a hooded coat."

"Who all saw it," Jess asked.

"Betty and Wanda were there. They saw the person too and were trying to speculate who it was."

"And I interviewed Betty and all the other merchants on Main, and not a one of them mentioned seeing anyone. Looks like I'll have to retrace my steps." He sighed. "I could sure use some help right about now."

"You know, I just thought of something," Rock said. "Have you had a chance to get to know Clarence Foster, one of our newest members?"

"Just in passing. I know he lost his wife last year. Rebecca helped out with some of the meals the Presbyterian Women prepared during that time. He lives out in the new Aldersgate subdivision, doesn't he?"

"Yes, and he worked as a detective in Jacksonville, Florida for close to thirty years before he retired. He recently told me he missed it and would like to get back into it part time. I'm sure he wouldn't mind brainstorming with you. He's a nice guy and with his background, he might see something that you're missing. He also needs a diversion."

"That's a great idea. I can probably squeeze enough out of the town council to pay him to do a little freelance work."

"I don't think he would take it. Before Teresa died, he even thought about volunteering over at the school as a traffic officer. I have a feeling he would be flattered if you approached him about it." He rambled around in his drawer. "Here's his card."

"See," Jess said. "I knew I could depend on you for help, even though you just passed me along to someone else."

"It's all about shutting one door and opening another," Rock said. When Jess looked at him in confusion, he laughed. "Just making a reference to my sermon Sunday. But seriously, I'm good at passing the buck. And it sounds like a fascinating case. Maybe when I grow up, I'll be a detective," he said with a grin.

"Maybe we could trade jobs." He stood up. "Nah," he said, "on second thought, I wouldn't wish that on you. My job's aggravating enough to make a preacher cuss."

Rock laughed. "Occasionally, so is mine."

CHAPTER 10

THE QUILTING ROOM

ain Street was getting back to normal and the murder was still a hot topic, but no longer consuming every conversation. Jess had gone back to each of the merchants and several of them remembered seeing the person Liz Clark had seen, but they all gave differing descriptions, with the exception of *tall and thin* and the black raincoat. Those were the only two things they agreed upon.

May complained that at least half the people in town had visited the back alley behind the small group of Main Street businesses just to get a glimpse of where a real murder took place. It was becoming a nuisance, she said. There were all kinds of theories making the rounds, anywhere from it being a gang-related murder to a drug deal gone bad. The police department had kept things quiet, too quiet for the curious minds about town, so when information was scarce, they tended to create their own, and soon, the tired old man who had walked into The Banty Hen Antique Shop was suddenly the mayor of some big town up north, an FBI agent looking for America's Most Wanted, or just someone who had died at the hands of a serial killer.

Meanwhile, inside The Banty Hen Antique Shop, preparations had been made for the first quilting club meeting. The new project had helped take Valerie's mind off the murder. She had brainstormed for days. Her first thought was that the group could all sit around the antique quilt rack Cap Price had brought into the shop a few months back. When he and Madge had combined households, they had nowhere to put it so they gave it to Sam. Sam had no idea what it was so he put a few old boards across the top and used it to display their old crocks and butter churns. Madge came in later and laughed, explaining to them how it was meant to be used. As many as eight women could sit comfortably around the frame, one on each end and three on each side. The quilt's three layers, the top, batting and backing material would be rolled between the slats and clamped down onto the frame. A needle and thread would be used to sew a running stitch by hand across the entire area to be quilted, rolling the quilt through the frame as they finished one area and started on another. It was a beautiful piece. The oak wood had a rich patina of warm earth tones and was about seven feet long by four feet wide. It was made almost like a table but with three crossbars instead of a table top. The end legs looked a little like saw horses with braces in between. While it had been perfect for quilters of a bygone era, Lydia had suggested that the group would be better off using sewing machines, at least on their first quilting projects. Maybe later they could tackle hand-stitching.

With Sam's help, she had made the place ready. The Christmas room had been cleaned out and whisked away upstairs in the attic by May's grandson. The quilting supplies had arrived, a newspaper notice had been published and the first meeting of the quilter's club had convened. Valerie had made a tray filled with dainty ham biscuits, English scones and a jar of homemade pear preserves. An electric teapot filled with hot tea and a big pitcher of iced tea rounded out the menu. She set it all up on a mahogany Hepplewhite sideboard covered in a tablecloth of fine Irish linen. Matching napkins and a stack of Haviland bread and butter plates completed the tablescape. She loved to set a pretty table and she beamed as the women exclaimed over it.

Sam voiced his surprise at the number of women who had shown up. An unlucky thirteen, he told Valerie when the last one had walked in the door. Sitting in the meeting she couldn't help but agree with him.

Cora Bradley had quickly asserted herself as the leading quilter by telling everyone she had been quilting since she was ten years old. No one knew exactly how old she was because she hadn't been born and raised in Park Place, but it was rumored she was seventy if she was a day.

"And exactly how long has that been?" Jenny Braswell asked, hoping Cora would slip up and tell them. No such luck.

"Long enough," she said, demurely brushing her newly dyed hair back behind her ears showing off her diamond earrings. Valerie didn't want to get things off to a bad start, so she interrupted. She had been researching the organizing of quilting clubs and had talked personally with Jane Simmons, the president of the club in Sparta. She would let them know the rules upfront because Jane told her that it could quickly become just a place to gossip and hang out if someone wasn't in charge. If Cora wanted to run things, fine and dandy, but only if she was elected. Anyone wanting to be the leader would put her name on the ballot and the election would be done not by a show of hands, but by secret ballot. Valerie quickly explained.

"Now who wants to have their name on the ballot for president of the club?" Cora, Lydia Swanson and Kay, the lady from Sun's Up Retirement Village all raised their hands.

Valerie gave Jenny some slips of paper to pass around. "Tell us a little about yourselves," Valerie said, "and why you want to be president."

"Why anyone would want to be the president of anything is beyond me," Maura McCarthy said. The local women laughed; they knew that Maura had always been nominated and elected to just about every committee at church until she'd finally got up the gumption to say no.

Each of the three women spoke for a few minutes, names were written on the slips of paper, and they were put in a box. Valerie and Rebecca Hamilton counted the ballots, and just like that, Lydia Swanson was the new club president. It was decided that Cora would be the treasurer and Kay would be the secretary.

When the meeting began, Madge Price raised her hand and brought up the name of the club for new business. "Valerie, I know you've put a lot of work into this and we all appreciate it. I've been wanting to take up quilting again for quite awhile but just didn't have the initiative to get started. I hate to say this, but you know how blunt I am. When I told Cap that I was going to The Banty Hen Quilter's Club's first meeting, he went into a fit of laughter. 'Like a bunch of old banty hens cackling and gossiping', he said. I wanted to punch him."

Valerie laughed. "I hadn't thought about that," she said. "I don't mind if the name is changed. I just thought since we were meeting here in the shop, it would make sense, but I see what you mean."

Maura spoke up. "I don't know. I kind of like The Banty Hen name."

Lydia got up to pour herself another glass of tea. "I've got it!" she said, holding up the pitcher of tea for the ladies to see. "How about Sweet Tea Quilting Bee. It has a nice ring to it."

"Hey, I like that," Jenny said. "We're a bunch of sweet tea junkies anyway. Look at what a job we've done on Valerie's tea pitcher. The tea's almost gone."

"Don't worry, I have more if we run out. I'll have Sam bring it in."

"If you do, we'll all be running for a bathroom break," Madge said. "I like the name too."

"Okay, what do you all think about the new name? Do we change it to the Sweet Tea Quilting Bee?" With a unanimous show of hands, including Valerie's, the name was changed.

Their next step was to pick a quilting pattern for their first lesson. Since six of the ladies present were first time quilters, they settled on a simple pattern in small dimensions - baby quilts. Valerie had a feeling it was going to be a slow go, and she could see from Lydia's expression that this wasn't quite what she had envisioned. Valerie wondered if maybe she should have put the notice in the paper asking for experienced quilters only, but then again, everyone had to start somewhere. She was pleased to see before the meeting ended, there was a spirit of camaraderie among the women, and the old quilters seemed to take the newbies in under their wings.

"Remember to bring your sewing machines next week. For those of you who don't have one, I'm sure we can make do with just a few. Also, Valerie and I have put together a sewing basket for each of you with the things you'll need. If you already have your supplies, don't feel obligated to take one. Those of you who do, please pay Valerie on the way out."

Everyone took a basket as they left. "I know I have all this stuff at home, but finding it is another matter," Madge said. "I don't know where anything is since I moved. I have at least fifteen boxes that I haven't even opened yet. Cap says to wait about a year and if I haven't needed something out of the boxes by then, just give the whole unopened box to the Hospice Re-sell Shop."

"That's not a bad idea," Maura said. "But I could never do that. I would be too curious to see what I had packed away."

They slowly drifted out, paying Valerie as they left. Lydia stayed on for a while. "I'll have to admit, Valerie, when I saw the show of hands of the women who had never quilted, I had a moment of trepidation. But then when I saw the enthusiasm in the room to learn something new, I thought what a great opportunity it is to carry on a tradition that so many Southern women have done before us. My grandmother taught my mother and my mother taught me, but in the last few decades with so many women working, there's been no time to pass it down. My own daughters aren't interested."

"Thanks for helping us out, Lydia. I'm looking forward to learning from someone who's had as much experience as you."

Lydia beamed. "Maybe we can have a quilt exhibit when we've all finished a quilt."

It was her turn to be excited. Maybe this was just what she and Sam needed to get people inside the shop. Getting them in the door was half the battle for a shopkeeper. A quilt exhibit would be good for the shop and for all the other businesses on Main Street.

***

Valerie pointed to the sign above the doorway to the back room. "Sam, you'll need to make a new sign."

"Why?" He looked hurt. "Is that one not good enough?"

"They changed the name. It's now the Sweet Tea Quilting Bee." She laughed. "Cap Price said our name sounded like a bunch of hens gathering, cackling and gossiping."

Sam puffed up. "Well, that old coot!"

"No, Sam, he's right. I like the new name. It sounds sort of..., well sweet."

Sam wasn't convinced. "I should get Cap Price to make the new sign," he said, and walked off in a huff. Valerie knew he would calm down after a bit and sure enough, about fifteen minutes later she heard the electric wood-burning tool spring to life. When he came out from the back, he was holding a slightly larger sign. He held it up for Valerie to see. The outline of a honey bee was burned into each corner. "Do you think I should put daisies on here too and brighten it up with a touch of white and yellow?"

"That would be amazing, dear!"

CHAPTER 11

COLUMBO

Rev Rock had been right. Clarence Foster was tickled as punch to be asked to help with the biggest murder case to ever happen in Park Place, or as the newspaper had said, the only murder case to ever happen in Park Place. When the murder story was printed in the paper, Clarence's first thought was that he would love to help solve the case, and lo and behold, here Jess Hamilton was asking him to do just that. Rev Rock had recommended him.

Teresa had known from the very beginning that Park Place Presbyterian was where they were meant to be. When the people there found out about her illness, they were warm and kind, even offering to cook meals and sit with her when Clarence had to run errands. He knew she would be happy he had joined and was in a special place where people genuinely cared about him. The generational makeup of the church was diverse and the children and youth programs were alive and well. He had just told his own grandchildren in Charlotte about the Bible School activities they were planning for the summer and they were excited about visiting. It was his opinion that a church would just shrivel up and die if there were no children to continue in the tradition of worship. Maybe it would be a good way to get his own daughter and son-in-law active in church again, especially when they saw how polite and friendly the other kids were. Teresa would have been pleased to see that.

And now, here he was, being offered another chance to do the work he loved best, solving crimes. Jess had explained that there wasn't much money in the coffers to pay him, but he quickly told him he would work on a volunteer basis. Anything to keep busy. He and Teresa had invested wisely and he had a good pension from the police department. He'd tried several hobbies but they just weren't as satisfying to his soul as what he'd been doing for half his life. He thought about the sermon Rev Rock had preached Sunday. Maybe God was opening a new door for him after all.

His first order of business would be to talk to the county coroner. He had an appointment with him on Thursday morning. For now, he would go over all the evidence, and as he looked at the folder in front of him, he realized there wasn't much. His second order of business was to re-interview any witnesses. Sometimes people didn't realize they had witnessed some small item that could be crucial to a case. Jess had already interviewed the Main Street merchants twice, but a new face asking the right questions could bring up new information. Jess had also mentioned a new nun in town. The only thing that could connect her at the moment was that she was tall and thin. There was probably no use at all to interview her, but he wouldn't leave any stone unturned. Anyway, that's what he was best at. His department buddies in Jacksonville had called him Columbo, because he kept hammering away until he got the information he wanted. He even took to wearing a tattered old raincoat, and after a while found that his confidence wasn't quite as good when he worked a case without it, but it sure was hot in Florida wearing one all the time. Maybe it was still in his closet. He would look when he got home, but he'd wager that Teresa had thrown it out in the trash when they moved. No big deal, he needed a new raincoat anyway.

***

Edmund Finley was the elected coroner for the county and worked in the basement of a building that had most recently been used as the zoning office. During his six years of service in the county, he had done several autopsies but this was his first murder victim from Park Place. Clarence had found out through his phone conversation with Mr. Finley that he was sixty years old and had also retired from a busy, highly stressful job in another state. He too had quickly become bored with retirement and decided to run for the office of coroner. Mr. Finley had worked as a forensic scientist in Chicago and had moved south for the warmer climate, like so many other retirees.

As he stepped into the coroner's office, Clarence's first thought was that he had good taste in music. A Beatles' soundtrack was playing in the background. After spending just a few minutes with Mr. Finley, he knew that the citizens had picked the right man for the job. He was extremely knowledgeable, and had already deducted, even before the autopsy, that the man's death was more than likely a reaction to the attack and not the attack itself.

"State law requires us to make every effort to find a next-of-kin to identify the body and if none are found, after ten days we can do the autopsy. I finally got the authorization and I have the report ready."

"If his assailant didn't kill him, how did he die?"

"He was literally frightened to death, and in my opinion the assailant is still responsible for the murder."

"I've heard of this, Edmund, but I've never worked a case where it's happened. Tell me about it."

"Please call me Ed." Clarence nodded. "The nervous system is a complex thing. It uses adrenaline to send signals to various part of the body to activate the fight-or-flight response. In large amounts, this chemical is toxic to the internal organs, especially the heart, and it can cause sudden death by way of a heart attack. That's what I've concluded happened to Mr. Gunther when his attacker put his hands around his throat. His airway was not damaged enough by the strangulation to cause his death."

"So, you think the murder was unintentional?"

"I'm afraid only the assailant can answer that one. He may have been intending to kill him anyway and the heart attack just made it easier."

"Hmm.... I guess it's up to us to find out, isn't it?"

"If you can catch the assailant."

"Don't worry, we'll get our man."

"That's another thing," Ed Finley said, "I'm not sure it's a man."

"Really? So, it could be a woman?" He was surprised. The thought that a woman may have tried to choke Mr. Gunther was not something he had seriously considered.

"I'm not saying that," he said. "The marks on the neck are consistent with thin hands. Not necessarily small hands, but slender ones. Of course, there are many men who have slender hands. Pianists, surgeons, artists, it's not a physical trait exclusive to women, but I'm just putting it out there that it's a possibility."

"Hmm.... That broadens the field of suspects, doesn't it? If we had any suspects in the first place. I've got to find a common denominator between the victim and the assailant."

"With your experience, I'm sure you will."

Clarence grinned. "They don't call me Columbo for nothin'."

"You don't even want to know all the things a forensic scientist gets called. Columbo? I liked that show. I heard Peter Falk died a couple years back."

"Oh yeah? I hadn't heard. What did he die from?"

Ed Finley grinned, eyeing the raincoat Clarence was wearing. "I think it was from never removing his raincoat," he said. Clarence laughed and Ed continued, "I'm just kidding; it was actually from cardiorespiratory arrest."

"As long as he wasn't frightened to death," Clarence said.

"Highly unlikely," Ed said with a chuckle. "By the way, good luck on the case. I'm glad they finally got Jess Hamilton some help. I hope they're paying you well."

"Strictly voluntary."

"I figured as much, Ed said. "I may as well be doing the same, no more than they're paying me, but I look at it this way; if I'm out of my wife's way, she doesn't make those long 'honey-do' lists that she made when I first retired."

Clarence smiled on the surface, but his thoughts were of Teresa. He would give anything if she was still alive to write a list of things for him to do. "I'll work with Jess as long as he needs me," he said.

"Here," Ed said, handing Clarence a legal sized piece of paper. "Pass along the results of the autopsy to Jess, if you will. He's been hounding me to death for it."

"Will do. It was nice talking with you. I haven't made many friends here yet. Maybe we can get together and play some golf."

"How about some fishing instead? I stink at golf. I bought a little boat and I fish on weekends. My wife won't go out with me, so maybe you could tag along sometime."

"I'd like that," Clarence said. "See you later." He walked up the basement steps leading outside. The sun was shining bright enough to make him want to whistle one of his favorite tunes by The Beatles. He'd accomplished a lot today. He'd made a new friend and now he had some new facts about the case. What he didn't know was that now he would have The Beatles' tune, *Here Comes the Sun* stuck in his head for days.

***

Clarence had given Jess a copy of the autopsy report and he spoke as he added it to the folder. "You know, I had actually played around with the idea that the cousin might be the assailant, or at least I did until she turned up missing with a possibility of foul play."

"That's a thought," Clarence said. "If they were fighting over the quilt, she had a motive."

"Apparently, someone else had a motive too. The Aberdeen police called today. They've been interviewing neighbors of Mr. Gunther and found out an interesting revelation."

"What's that?"

"Mr. Gunther liked to play the horses and he owed a loan shark quite a bit of money. The neighbor in the apartment next to his heard him arguing with someone the day before he disappeared. The person had demanded the money, even threatening Mr. Gunther's life if he didn't get it. Mr. Gunther told him that he had just inherited an expensive quilt and when he auctioned it off, he would pay him what he owed him plus interest."

"How much did he owe him?"

"$1,000."

"The same amount Gunther tried to sell the quilt for to the antique shop owners."

"Exactly," Jess said. "The surveillance cameras outside Gunther's apartment building show a tall, thin man entering and then leaving the apartment at the approximate time it was ransacked. The neighbor knew the time because she remembered that she was aggravated that she couldn't hear *The Price is Right* on TV for all the noise next door. The detective said the apartment walls are so thin, an intruder would have easily been heard by the neighbor. Too bad she didn't call the police."

"She probably wanted to get back to *The Price is Right*. It's a shame that today's typical mentality is such that if it's happening to someone else, they don't want to get involved."

"And it creates a cold crime scene if it's not reported right away," Jess said.

"Exactly, and a tall, thin man could have slender hands." Clarence was tapping his pen on his temple, a habit he'd acquired from his years as a detective. "I guess the next question is, what does the loan shark look like?"

Jess smiled. "tall and thin - I'll see if I can get a photo of him. His name is Arlo Balbini, and according to his employer, he took several days off during the time this all happened. Trouble is, the Aberdeen police have interviewed him and says he has an alibi. On the days leading up to the murder, he was home with the flu..., and his wife is his alibi."

"That's not airtight in my opinion."

"Mine either, but we need more evidence."

"Any luck in locating the missing cousin?"

"No, not yet, but we do know that she withdrew as much cash as possible from an ATM, $400. The camera at the ATM wasn't good quality, but there was someone standing behind her. It's impossible to tell if they were with her forcing her to withdraw it or just waiting in line to use the ATM."

"Let me guess. A tall, thin man?"

Jess nodded. "You guessed right."

"Well I can tell you right now, Jess. Your first murder case is anything but open and shut. What a tangled web."

"Amen."

"I plan to go over to St. Gabriel's and talk to the nun at some point. Do you have any objections if I go back and talk to the folks in the shops on Main Street again? With my ugly mug in their face, they may think of something else they saw."

"Knock yourself out. I can't wait to see your reaction when you've talked to all of them, though. You'll be just as confused as I am. Truthfully, I'm glad you're up to the challenge. We just don't have enough staff or experience to work this kind of case. Sometimes I feel like my team is an Andy Taylor / Barney Fife kind of outfit right out of Mayberry."

"Don't sell yourself short," Clarence said. "You seem to be on top of things. I can just save you some legwork. Do you have a desk I can work from here in the station?"

"I beat you to the punch," Jess said. "Yes, there's a room down the hall that we have a few file cabinets in, but nothing else. I got a desk and office chair from Kit's consignment shop this morning. I was going to buy it, but when I told her what it was for, she gave it to me. It's not much, but it'll serve the purpose."

"Perfect. Could I make copies of the case folder?"

"Heather did that this morning. Your copy of the file is on top of your desk already."

CHAPTER 12

FOR MERCY'S SAKE!

"**S**am, I can't get the key in the door. See if you can do it."

It was Monday morning and Valerie and Sam both had their arms full. Valerie had spread the word about the quilter's club and Mabel Watkins gave her four bags of scrap material at church on Sunday to donate to the club. Her eyes were too old and tired, she said, and she just didn't have the patience to quilt anymore. It was old material but it would be good for practice.

Sam put the two bags he was carrying on the brick pavers leading up to the back door of the shop. "Here, I'll try," he said, taking the key from her and inserting it into the keyhole. "Hmm.... It's not working for me either. I need my glasses." He pulled his reading glasses out of his shirt pocket, and leaned over, trying again. "Hey, it's been jimmied," he said, taking the key back out of the hole and inspecting the lock. "It looks like someone jammed a screwdriver in here and stripped the keyhole. Wonder who could have done that?"

"And why didn't our alarm system work?"

Sam gritted his teeth and sighed. "Because someone forgot to set it Saturday," he said.

"Don't blame me," Valerie said indignantly. "You're the one who locked up."

"I wasn't blaming you," he said. "I was talking about myself. I'm the one who forgot. You remember, we were in a rush to close because that man looking for fishing lures came back right before closing time and we were late for our dinner reservations."

"Oh dear," she said. "At least it doesn't look like they were successful breaking in. This old back door is like a bank vault. We're lucky they didn't get in." She looked at him thoughtfully and shook her head. "No, luck has nothing to do with it. It's a blessing, isn't it?"

"Yes, it is. You know this building was a bank at one time, right after the general store closed. I suppose it had to be a strong door because of that."

"I think you need to call Jess. He said if anything suspicious happened to let him know."

"It seems like a waste of time since they didn't steal anything, but I guess you're right."

***

"No, you did absolutely the right thing," Jess said, as he wrote up the report.

Clarence was busy taking notes, but stopped and turned to face Sam and Valerie. "I've been planning to stop by and talk to the two of you anyway," he said. Sam looked at the new man suspiciously.

Jess noticed the room was suddenly quiet. He looked up and saw the impasse. "I'm sorry, Sam," he said. "You too, Valerie. I was so absorbed with the attempted break-in, I forgot to introduce you. This is Clarence Foster, a retired detective who has offered to help me out on this case. He's got a lot more experience with violent crimes than I do."

Sam looked relieved and held his hand out. Clarence took it and smiled. "It's my fault too," he said. "I just started blabbing and you had no idea who I was. I told Jess I want to interview everyone on Main Street to see if anyone saw something, maybe something they didn't think was important at the time or relevant to the case."

Valerie had been checking out his raincoat. "A real live Columbo," she said.

"So I've been called," he said, a little embarrassed, but pleased that she'd noticed.

"Should we be worried that you're going to hound us day and night?" she said, laughing.

He raised his eyebrow and grinned. "Only if you're guilty, Ma'am."

It was Sam's turn to laugh. "If I had been one of his suspects, I would have confessed even if I wasn't guilty to get the man off my back."

"Are you going to dust for fingerprints?" Valerie asked.

"Normally not for an attempted break-in," Jess said, "but since it's a possibility it has something to do with the death of Mr. Gunther, we will. I doubt we'll find anything since you both had your hands all over the lock trying to open it. But we'll compare any fingerprints we get with a national criminal database and see if we find a match."

"Will y'all excuse me while I go get prepared for our ladies? This is the the day of our quilting bee and they'll be here in forty-five minutes."

"Sure, go ahead," Jess said. "Oh, wait. Clarence said he wanted to interview the two of you." He looked at the detective.

"That's okay," Clarence said. "I'll talk to Sam and then come back later today after I've had a chance to talk to some of the other merchants on Main. We'll be out of your way before your quilters come in, won't we, Jess?"

"Yes, I'll dust for fingerprints while Clarence talks to Sam."

"Actually, Jess, I need Sam to come help me set up the chairs. Or if all three of you big, strong men will help, it can be done in no time." She flashed her biggest smile and all three jumped up at once. Jess smiled as they moved the antique rockers and side chairs in a semi-circle and thought to himself how quickly men move when sucker-punched by the smile of a sweet Southern Belle.

***

Valerie listened as Lydia brought the meeting to order and got on with the business at hand. "Ladies, I've given some thought to how we need to proceed and I think our next step is to pair the newbies with the oldies."

"Where do I fit in," Valerie asked. "I'm a newbie quilter in an oldie body." Everyone laughed.

"And me?" It was Holly, Maura's daughter-in-law speaking. "I grew up sitting at my mother's knee during her quilting sessions at our church. I had made my own quilt by the time I was twelve and I still have the quilt - it's on Abby's bed now."

"We'll consider you an oldie just this once", Valerie said. "As a matter of fact, I would love to be partnered with you."

"That's fine," Lydia said. "We have some bad news though. I heard from Cora Bradley this week and she's having to drop out of the club for now. Harold's mother is beginning to need round-the-clock care and since he only has two sisters, Cora needs to step in and help them. I had planned to just supervise and let the twelve of you work in pairs, but with Cora gone, there will only be eleven of you, an uneven number. That means I'll partner with someone to make it an even six pairs. On this project, we'll use some of the fabric that was so generously donated by Mabel Watkins, but not all of it is suitable for baby quilts. We'll purchase the rest from Valerie. She's giving us a huge discount; much less than we could buy it elsewhere. And if you oldies don't mind, we'll let the newbies have the finished product when you finish since they've never quilted anything on their own before." They all nodded in agreement. "Do we want to discuss what our next project is or wait until we've finished this one?"

"I can see so many possibilities," Holly said. "Some of the ladies from church brought quilts to the hospital when I was in there so long after the accident. I remember waking up from the coma surrounded by beautiful quilts. There was one on my bed, two draped on the chairs in the room, and even a quilted wall-hanging on the hospital room wall, an angel quilt. I felt like I'd died and gone to heaven. Maybe we could do that for all the seriously ill patients. Just a simple quilt would cheer up an otherwise dreary room."

Mary Beth, one of the youngest members spoke up. "That's a great idea, but since we've decided to make baby quilts this time and since I'm a newbie, I would love to donate my finished quilt to the nursery at the hospital. Wouldn't it be nice to donate enough for all their cribs so that each new little baby could be wrapped in a cozy quilt made by ladies in the community who will love and cherish the babies as they grow? Park Place is one of those places that truly lives out 'it takes a village to raise a child'. Our town is our own little slice of heaven." The other quilters quickly expressed their approval to donate their quilts to the nursery too.

"That's the spirit," Lydia said. "The other quilting club I belong to makes at least one quilt a year and donates it to a worthwhile charity to be auctioned at a fundraiser. I'm sure you have many worthwhile causes here in Park Place."

Valerie heard Sam clear his throat and cough at the doorway. She looked up to see him standing there waiting to get their attention. She smiled at him. "Did you need something, Sam?"

"Are y'all accepting new members?" He didn't wait for an answer and stood aside for another person to enter. Valerie was surprised to see the nun who had visited the store before. She walked in the room and the conversation stopped and everyone stared. There was total silence until Holly's thimble dropped and the sound of it on the hardwood floor made them all jump.

"I'm sorry if I interrupted your meeting." The nun looked embarrassed and just stood there.

"Oh my, where are our manners," Valerie said hurriedly and walked over to where she stood. She started to put her arm around her shoulder, but realized she was much taller and linked arms with her instead. "We were so intent on our future projects, and two of our members had just been speaking of heaven and here a nun walks through the door. For mercy's sake! You're more than welcome to join us. You've been in the shop before. Sister Margaret, I believe?"

"Yes, thank you. I've always been interested in quilting, but this is the first placement I've ever had where I'll have some free time. I thought I would give it a try until we get busier with the homeless shelter project." She looked around the room and didn't see any extra chairs. "If you have room, that is?"

Lydia spoke up. "We're glad to have you Sister Margaret. With you joining the group, we'll have an even number for pairing up and I can supervise like I'd planned to do."

Valerie turned to her husband who was still standing by the door. "Sam, would you bring in an extra chair while we fill our new member in on what we're doing?" The raised eyebrow look she gave Sam made him wonder what he'd done wrong. He shrugged his shoulders at her questioning glare.

"Of course, dear. I'll be right back." He came back in a few seconds later with a chair from a dining room set. "That's all we have that I could move easily," he said.

"That's perfect," Valerie said. "This will fit my back much better than the other one. Sister Margaret, how about taking my chair so I can sit in this one." Sam knew that Valerie's favorite chair was the one she was giving up, but it was just like her to think of someone else's comfort before her own.

Lydia and the others explained to Sister Margaret the idea of presenting the baby quilts they would be making to the nursery wing of the Park Place General Hospital and caught her up on the discussions thus far. Then she and Valerie opened the bags of quilt scraps and the seasoned quilters helped the new ones choose coordinating colors for their quilts. Valerie gave each team a bag to put them in, and Lydia started the first lesson.

"We'll start with the simplest quilting pattern - an X on a square. You've picked your colors and next you'll cut them into squares. Before we leave today, you can get your oldie quilter to explain how that's done and you can divide them up and each take some home to cut before we meet next week. Any questions?"

Mary Beth put her hand in the air. "How do we know what size squares to cut?"

"Your partner will tell you based on the pattern we've chosen. Anything else?" No one else spoke up so Lydia continued. "We have a few more things to add to your sewing baskets. They were included in the cost of your baskets but Valerie didn't have them in stock at the time. Each bag in front of you holds fabric scissors, packs of size 8 and size 10 needles, a needle threader, a seam ripper, thread conditioner, a pin cushion with quilt pins, a rotary cutter and board, marking pencils and two thimbles. One thimble is the standard cuff metal and the other is made of leather. We also have some quilting hoops and small frames to hold the fabric while you stitch." Valerie started handing out the bags, and getting an extra basket from the back for Sister Margaret.

"And for those of you who haven't quilted before, we'll go over exactly what makes up a quilt. First you have the colorful top part of the quilt which is simply pieces of fabric sewn together to create the pieced block." She held up a twin-size quilt that she had finished except for sewing on the border. "I'm making this one for my grandson." She passed it around and everyone oohed and aahed over it. When she got it back, she held it up again.

"Next you have the batting which is the cushioning layer that makes it a quilt, otherwise you would have just two layers of fabric which wouldn't be very warm and cuddly, would it? It also gives definition to the quilting stitches. Then you have the backing fabric which is made from one fabric pattern. It can be solid, patterned or floral. The floral and patterned fabric pieces are much more forgiving than the solid when you don't want your quilting stitches to show up on the back." She gave a few more instructions and then turned it over to the teams to go over what size squares to cut. Forty minutes later, they each had what they needed to continue working at home folded neatly in their baskets and were walking out the door. Valerie's stomach was growling and she was glad to see the last of them leave.

Sam was spreading a liberal glob of Duke's Mayonnaise on four slices of white bread when Valerie finally returned to the back office. "Ham or turkey?" he asked.

"Turkey," she answered.

"Okay, I won't put any mustard on yours then. You want apple slices on it?" She nodded and he finished making the sandwiches while she got ice from the refrigerator and poured the leftover tea in the glasses. They sat at the small table to eat.

"By the way, why the funny look when I brought in the nun, Valerie? Did I do something wrong?"

"I'm sorry, Sam. My first reaction was that things would be so stuffy and formal having a nun in the group, but I was wrong. I think it will work out just fine. She seems nice enough and doesn't act very nun-like."

Sam smiled at her. "And what exactly is a nun supposed to act like?"

"I really don't know since I've never been around one."

"What else could I have done, thrown her out?"

"No, of course not. It did take up a lot of time explaining things all over again. We didn't get a lot done. I do think we should close the membership until we get this project done and start on a new one." She took a bite of her sandwich and washed it down with her drink. "It was odd, though," she said. "She seemed to know a lot more about quilting than she let on. She didn't hesitate when choosing fabrics that matched and she seemed familiar with all the quilting tools. I noticed that she tried on the leather thimble on the correct finger. Most new quilters have no idea what finger it goes on."

"Maybe she's seen people quilting but just hasn't done it herself."

"Maybe..."

What was the big deal about quilting anyway, Sam wondered? Let the ladies hash it out. He didn't want any part of it.

Sam was cleaning off the glass counter when Clarence Foster walked back in the store. "How was your day? Did you find any new clues?" he asked.

He sighed. "This ain't Jacksonville," he said, shaking his head.

Sam laughed. "I could have told you that."

The detective laid several items down on the counter Sam had just finished cleaning. "Whatcha got there?" Sam asked.

"A stash," he said. He picked one thing at a time and held it up. "This is a complimentary salted caramel brownie from the new bakery." He set it down and picked up another. "And these are stainless steel screws Mr. Crowder talked me into buying when I mentioned I had a little project to do around the house."

Sam smiled. Just like Junie! He'd never gone into Crowder's Feed and Seed without Junie talking him into buying something. He looked at the long narrow box. "May's Flower Shop?"

"Oh yes. May had some tulips left over from a wedding she did over the weekend so when I told her I was coming back here, she sent them for Valerie." Clarence grinned. It was easy to see he was amused. "You can get a lot of mileage out of the flowers, Sam. Women love tulips. I won't say a word about her giving them to me."

There was one more bag, a pink one. "And this," he said, "is from the post office. A loaf of bread for my chickens that I don't have." He pulled out another item. "Here's a book of forever stamps because Betty swears the cost of stamps will be going back up soon, and a book by a local author who Betty says wrote the book about her, and I can see why because she is quite a character. She insisted that I buy it, something about supporting local artists. How could I resist? He reached in his front pants pockets and pulled them inside out, and in mock indignation, held them up empty for Jess to see. "See, I'm $20 poorer just because I stepped inside the post office."

Sam had been trying not to laugh but at the thought of this serious-minded detective trying to talk seriously with Betty made him shake with laughter.

Clarence joined in. "This is a colorful little town you've got here. I would move here in a heartbeat if we hadn't already bought our house in Aldersgate."

"You would have a hard time finding property for sale here unless someone died," Sam said. "The people who end up here never want to leave."

"I don't blame them," Clarence said. "But it's sure not a good place to ask questions. Everybody was so busy asking me questions, like where I'm from and who's my mama, I couldn't get a word in edgewise." He shook his head. "I've never seen anything like it." He looked around the shop. "How was your wife's quilting club meeting," he asked. "Did we pull in enough chairs?"

"We did until the nun came in," Sam said.

Clarence's head jerked up with interest. "The nun?"

CHAPTER 13

A NEW DEVELOPMENT

Clarence pulled into the parking lot of St. Gabriel's Catholic Church and parked close to what he figured must be the old rectory, now the homeless shelter. The door was open, so he walked in expecting to encounter Sister Margaret, the new assistant Father Thomas had told him about when he called to make an appointment. "Just come on out", he'd said. "You don't need an appointment. We've been busy all morning sprucing things up a bit."

He hadn't told the priest that he specifically wanted to see the nun when he called. It would have drawn too much attention. He had simply told him he wanted to see the new shelter, which was also true.

He heard a voice call out, "Can I help you?" He looked around, and finally saw someone at least eight feet up on a rickety ladder. It was a natural reaction for him to run over and try to steady the ladder since it looked as if it would fall at any moment. "Oh, I'm fine," a feminine voice said. "But I'll come down because I can see I'm making you nervous."

He held the ladder as she made her way down, and when she stepped off the last rung and turned to face him, he took a sharp intake of breath. He had never seen anyone more beautiful than the woman standing right then and there in front of him, even though she wore a pair of overalls and t-shirt with paint splatters all across the front. Not a word would come out of his mouth as she looked at him expectantly.

"Cat got your tongue?" she asked with a shy smile.

"What? Oh, uh, yes, I think so," he said as he returned her smile. What was wrong with him? His heart was pounding away and he felt almost giddy. Then he felt a stab of guilt. Teresa had been gone but a year and here he was acting like a moonstruck teenager. He shook his head, trying to come to his senses.

"I'm Clarence Foster," he said. "I talked to Father Thomas earlier and he said it was okay if I came by."

"I'm Maggie, it's nice to meet you, Clarence Foster," she said. There was something warm about the way she said it which made Clarence feel she really meant it. "Father Thomas is in his office up at the church right now. I can show you the way, or is there something I can help you with?"

Yes, you can fall in love with me, he thought, and for a minute he blushed, wondering if he had said it out loud. "I'm actually looking for Sister Margaret," he said. "Can you tell me where she is?"

"Guilty as charged," she said, with a mischievous grin on her face. When he gave her an incredulous look, she said, "Well, I can't very well paint in long black flowing robes, can I?"

He laughed. "No, I guess that would be awkward." He felt disappointment and relief. He certainly didn't need to get tangled up in a relationship so soon after Teresa's passing. And being around a nun was safe. Or was it? He wasn't going to hang around long enough to find out. Besides, there couldn't be a connection with the case.

"I just came by to see the shelter," he said. "I'm working part-time for the police department. I wanted to check it out so we can recommend it when we pick up someone who may be homeless."

"Or in need of a good meal," she said. We'll be serving meals too if there's a need. Come on, I'll show you around."

"Oh no, that's okay. You're busy painting. I'll wait until Father Thomas has a chance to show me around sometime."

"Nonsense," she said. "I need a break anyway. Just wait here until I go into the kitchen and wipe the paint off my face and hands." She looked down at her clothes. "The rest of me is hopeless!"

She had a small frame and wasn't nearly as tall as Cliff had said. Of course, Cliff was only about 5'9", so his idea of tall would be different. She turned on her heels to go. "On second thought, you'll want to see the kitchen too, so just follow me."

He watched her as she leaned over the sink and splashed water on her face. She grabbed a paper towel and rubbed it across her face, then dried her hands. When she looked back up at him and smiled, he felt his knees were going to buckle. He said a silent prayer as he followed her from room to room. "Lord, take away this feeling from me. She belongs to you." He felt better, and was finally able to carry on a conversation without stammering and blushing and found that she was just as intelligent as she was pretty.

"You said you're working three days a week at the police department?"

"Yes, unless they need me more often."

"As you can tell, we could use a hand here with the painting. We were hoping to get some of our parishioners to volunteer but everyone's either too busy or not interested in the project. If you ever feel like volunteering, come on by and bring friends. No need for an appointment."

"I might just do that," he said, but he knew full well it would be his undoing if he did. This was all quite new to him. It was time for a discussion with someone he could trust. Jess? No, he wouldn't understand. He immediately thought of Rev Rock, but decided against it. What he needed was a heartfelt discussion with God. Yes, prayer, and he admitted to himself that he hadn't done nearly enough of it lately.

***

"There's been a new development." Jess said after Clarence got back from St. Gabriel's.

Clarence pulled a chair closer to Jess's desk. "Good, I'm not having much luck here in town. What is it?"

"The Annapolis police tried a new angle. Since they haven't been able to find Mr. Gunther's cousin Amelia, they tried to find out what they could about the aunt who passed away recently."

Clarence nodded his head. "That's a good place to start."

"Her name was Marilee Bayley and she was the last owner of the quilt. Since she's passed away, her attorney is no longer tied to attorney-client privilege rules, so he cooperated and told the police she had written several wills in the year prior to her death. He felt she was playing one cousin against the other so they would be at her beck and call. One will would make Mr. Gunther the recipient of the quilt and the next one would leave it to his cousin. She made a change to the will about two months before her death leaving the quilt to the Baltimore Museum of the Arts without telling either of them. Even though they each inherited an equal share of the estate, an aging home in a rundown neighborhood, it was peanuts compared to the value of the quilt. She told the attorney that neither of them deserved it. They would just sell it to make some quick money and she knew the museum would appreciate it. The poor condition of the home would hinder a quick sale on the property, so if the heirs needed quick cash, it would be a long time coming."

"How were those two related to Mrs. Bayley?"

"Mr. and Mrs. Bayley had no children of their own, but Mrs. Bayley had two sisters who each had one child. Both of her sisters have passed away, leaving Horace and Amelia her only surviving relatives."

"Were the two of them close? Sometimes cousins can be as close to each other as siblings."

"According to Mrs. Bayley's neighbors, the two of them were always bickering and clamoring for their aunt's attention."

"How did Horace Gunther come into possession of the quilt?"

"That's the mystery," Jess said. "Apparently both he and Amelia had keys to old Mrs. Bayley's house since they had helped with her caregiving for the last year. One of them took it, but since one of them is dead and the other is missing, no one knows which one."

"There could be several different scenarios," Clarence said. "But the ones I've thought of have holes in them. We need to know what role, if any, the tall, thin man, presumably the loan shark, plays in this."

"At this time, the scenarios seem to be one of the following. Aunt dies, Amelia steals her quilt, Horace ransacks her house and finds it and leaves town. Amelia ransacks his house to look for it, finds Horace and the quilt gone, somehow tracks him down and gets into a scuffle with him in the alleyway behind the dumpster. But where is she and how on earth would she have tracked him to Park Place? Yeah, there are holes alright and much too complicated. I'm not even going into the next scenario because I see what you mean. We need to find Amelia and check out the loan shark."

Clarence laughed. "And the only witness we have of anything is Horace's neighbor hearing the noise and the security video showing the tall, thin man. But you know what? I'm ready for a challenge. Are all the phone numbers you've called in Maryland inside the folder?"

"Yes," Jess said. "All of them. Even the attorney's. What are your thoughts? Could I have missed something?"

"I just want to check a new angle. We know the next-of-kin for Mrs. Bayley, but how about her deceased husband. Which side of the family was the quilt passed down from, and does he have any relatives still living and if so, did he leave a will that could supercede Mrs. Bayley's?"

"See," Jess said. "This is out of my league. I'm so glad you showed up on my doorstep."

Clarence smiled. "I've got a few years and a lot of caseloads behind me," he said. "One more thing before I go to my office; I went out to St. Gabriel's and met the mysterious new nun today."

"Really, what was she like?"

"Tall and slim," he said with a wry grin.

Jess's eye popped open in surprise. "You're kidding me, right? Cliff said the same thing."

Clarence laughed at the expression on his new friend's face. "I couldn't help myself. No, really. She's not that tall; slim, yes; attractive, yes; possibility of being criminally involved, no. She certainly doesn't look like any nun I've ever seen."

"Hmm, Cliff said she was attractive too. You sure she's not just masquerading as a nun?"

"I don't know any more than you do, but she's not attractive in a showy or suggestive kind of way. She's so unpretentious, she doesn't even realize how pretty she is."

"Well, she must have made an impression on you. You sound like you're a little bit smitten with her."

"Don't go there; she's a nun, remember?"

"Sorry, Clarence, I didn't mean to imply..."

"Oh no, I didn't take it that way." He grinned. "I'm just trying to remind myself that she's a nun and totally off limits, as if I was ready for that sort of thing anyway."

"You will be one day," Jess said. "How old are you anyway? I can get away with asking you because you're volunteering and it won't be age discrimination if I ask."

Clarence laughed. "And you can't fire me. I'll be fifty-two in August, Jess. I retired with twenty-eight years on the force, starting just as soon as I graduated from law enforcement school. Teresa and I met in high school; she was a year younger - just fifty when she died last year, far too young."

"Yes, far too young. Rebecca and I are in our forties and I can't imagine anything happening to her, but your wife was only a few years older. Goes to show you never know when your time will be up. I'm sorry."

A minute passed with each of them lost in their reflections. Clarence was the first to break the silence. "Tall and slim; we seem to have found the common denominator anyway. In a country of obesity, everyone under suspicion so far is tall and slim. How many tall and slim people do we have so far?"

There are a few here in town anyway, but I've known them for years and there's no way they could have connections with Mr. Gunther. Then there's Russell Walker, a newcomer who works the lunch counter at Carter's Drugstore; there's the loan shark who Gunther owed money to; Gunther's cousin Amelia, according to the missing person's description; a stranger who went into the antique store looking for old fishing lures; and a woman who also visited The Banty Hen asking about old quilts. And get this, that woman had a heart shaped birthmark on her forehead."

"Like Horace Gunther had on his shoulder based on the coroner's report," Clarence said.

"Exactly."

"Could any of them be one and the same?"

"You mean like a man disguised as a woman? Anything's possible. Of course, it would be easier for a man to disguise himself as a woman than vice-versa, wouldn't it?"

"Not necessarily," Clarence said. "A man's hat or ballcap might easily pull off a good disguise for a woman, especially if she was thin anyway."

"And remember, the coroner specifically said it could be a woman because the marks on the neck were consistent with slender hands."

"That's right. We can't rule out a woman. Listen, we can beat this to death if we keep thinking of the possibilities, so I think I'll head to my office to look over the folder and make a few phone calls. I've been out in the field so much, I haven't had time to break in my new office. I haven't even checked. Is there a landline in there?"

"No, but the cell phone service is decent. If you have trouble getting out, we'll get the phone company in here and install one. We have a laptop you can take if you need to look for something online. It picks up the WiFi signal from Heather's office."

"Thanks Jess, you've thought of everything. I feel like I'm back at work."

"And I'm glad to have you!"

CHAPTER 14

THE HEART WON'T LIE

Maggie Mead sat at a small desk tucked in the corner of what was once the sitting room of the old rectory. She had just finished meeting with a donor who wanted to see the facilities before he made his mind up to give to the shelter. She couldn't wait to tell Father Thomas that the donor had been impressed with the operation and left, but not before writing a check for $4000 to cover the utility bills for a year.

She picked up a file folder and fanned herself with it. It was an unseasonably warm day but not quite hot enough yet for air conditioning. She had opened the windows to let some fresh air into the musty house turned homeless shelter, but instead of cooling the office, the sun beaming from the west into the open windows had made it warmer. Early April should be bringing cool showers she thought, or at least it usually did in the mid-Atlantic states. She kept forgetting she was in a subtropical climate. She hated to think what the weather would be like come summer.

She loosened the white band on her forehead and carefully removed the black veil from her head. She wondered how other nuns could wear them all the time, especially in the summer. With the starched collar loosened around her neck she felt much better. She was grateful that the Dominican Order she belonged to finally allowed the Sisters in the mission community to wear regular clothes unless they were conducting official church business. Not so much in the formation community, but the dress code was still more lenient than other orders of the church.

She folded the black veil carefully and laid it upon the desk. If someone came in she would hear them through the open foyer and don the headgear once again. It was a relief not have to wear her habit when she was doing physical labor, and she'd been doing a lot of that lately.

A key, then a tug of the handle opened the stubborn desk drawer and revealed a thin file folder inside. She pulled the few documents out of the folder and sat there staring at them. Looking out from the first photo was a younger version of the dearly departed Horace Gunther. She had written across the bottom 'deceased'. She put it aside and looked at the other photo. A middle-aged woman with a narrow face and wide eyes stared back at her. She studied the other features. Medium length salt and pepper hair softened the prominent features somewhat, but the angular shape of her nose and the thin line of eyebrows and curl of her lips gave away the fact that she was not a soft or sweet person, a fact she had already gathered over the years about Amelia Reinhart. And then there was that birthmark.

With the clumsy head attire now thrown upon the desk, she reached up and patted her own hair. The moment she'd noticed a few strands of gray peeking through she had immediately made a trip to the drug store and purchased a honey brown hair dye almost identical to her own hair color. Not that she had anything against gray hair, she just didn't want it on her own head. After all, she was only in her late thirties. Gray hair had come too quickly and could wait a few years. It wasn't a normal practice among nuns in her Order to color their hair, but it wasn't prohibited. Of course, it would be different if she dyed it a color that would bring undue attention to herself, like a garishly red or an unnatural blonde color.

It was bad enough that she was so blasted thin. She had tried her best to gain weight over the years, but it was in her genes to be the size of a toothpick. Her mother always told her that she was the spitting image of her father and the photos she'd seen of him verified it, only she had her mother's rounder face and pleasing features. Her father had been killed in action at the tail end of the Vietnam War, only a few days after her mother had given birth to his baby girl. She wondered how her life would have turned out if he had lived. She remembered the day when her mother decided to move away from the only father figure she had known up until that point, her grandfather. It had broken her heart to leave the home of her grandparents, her father's parents, where she and her mom had lived while he was off fighting a war that no one seemed to understand. They had stayed on there until Maggie was seven years old. She hadn't understood at the time, but now she did. Her mom was young and living with her dead husband's parents was awkward if she ever wanted to date again. She worked hard and after saving some money, was finally financially able to move.

Their move had been hard on her grandparents, but at least Maggie got to visit them each summer. Her father had only one brother, her Uncle Al, and he and his wife never had children, so Maggie was the only grandchild.

Al's wife was always jealous of Maggie, because her grandparents made it clear that Maggie would inherit all the family treasures, however meager they seemed at the time.

Her mother remarried and her stepfather was kind to her. He was Catholic and she went to Catholic schools until she finished high school, then on to Mercy College in Toledo where she first felt the calling to become a nun.

She fiddled with the stiff collar and started to button it again, but changed her mind. She sighed and picked her rosary beads up from the desk, passing each one carefully through her fingers.

She had been faithful to her calling for the last fifteen years, but lately she had become restless and wondered again about the path she had taken. Had it been the right one? Yes, without a doubt the vocation God had called her to had been the right one, but now she was wondering if He was calling her to another. Lately, she had been having dreams that she was a mother, holding a tiny baby in her arms. It was a comforting feeling and when she awoke, she found herself longing to hold a baby of her own. Maybe all women felt that way at her age when their fertile years were passing quickly by. The old biological clock ticking away. But why would God be putting this upon her heart? It was all so confusing. She had lived a happy life in the community of the church and she had learned so much. Surely this was just a fickle moment and would pass if she immersed herself in prayer. Her mind drifted once again to yesterday, and the good-looking detective who made her heart beat a little faster. "What are you calling me to do, God," she pleaded out loud. "Is it time for me to leave? Please give me some answers and some peace!"

It didn't help that at the same time she was dealing with another problem. It had never bothered her much that her uncle and aunt had kept her grandparent's treasures, despite the will's stipulations. What good were material possessions to her in the calling she had chosen anyway, but there was one item she had always wanted, simply for nostalgic reasons. Ever since the lawyers of her deceased uncle had called her, she had struggled with what she should do. She really should go to the police and give them the information she had. The detective had seemed nice enough and was easy to talk to. But something was holding her back.

She looked through the folder one more time, then put it back in the drawer and locked it with the small key she had found taped to the underside. She slipped the key into the pocket of her loose habit and got up from the chair to turn on the TV that had been donated to the shelter for the transient residents when they arrived. It was noon; there should be some weather reports. Maybe there would be some relief in sight for the heat. She certainly hoped so, or she would have to go purchase a lighter-weight habit, or not wear one at all which was what more and more nuns of her Order were now doing. The habit which she had once worn proudly as a symbol of her vows now felt more like an albatross around her neck.

With her back to the door and the sound of the TV as she turned up the volume, she didn't hear Father Thomas as he slipped in the front door, nor did she see the shock on his face when she started singing and swaying along with Reba McIntyre as she was being featured on the mid-day entertainment report. Nor did he see the tears that slipped unchecked down her cheek while she sang.

> "Cause the heart won't lie
> Sometimes life gets in the way
> But there's one thing that won't change
> I know I've tried
> The heart won't lie
> You can live your alibi
> Who can see you're lost inside a foolish disguise
> The heart won't lie."

Father Thomas did an about face and hurried out the door of the rectory much faster than he came in, closing the door softly behind him. What in the world were they teaching these nuns nowadays, he wondered? He was in such a dither, he almost ran into the man walking up the steps to the rectory. "Oops! Forgive me," he said. "I wasn't paying attention." He stopped and gathered his thoughts. "I'm Father Thomas. Is there anything I can help you with?"

"That's okay, I get in a hurry sometimes myself. I'm Clarence Foster and I talked to you by phone a few days back."

He checked the man over. Wearing an old t-shirt and coveralls, he looked like a painter. He didn't remember talking to a painter, but the name sounded familiar. "Oh yes, I see you've come to paint. Go right on in. Uh, on second thought, when you stick your head in the door, give a little shout-out to let Sister Margaret know you're on your way in. I wouldn't want to frighten her."

"I will," he said, and walked up to the door. "Sister Margaret?" he called out. "Are you here?"

Father Thomas listened and heard the Sister answer. "Yes, I'll be right there." He was relieved. He wouldn't want anyone walking in on a dancing nun. It would be downright embarrassing.

Clarence walked on in, shutting the door behind him. He was nervous and was now second-guessing his decision to come back. The TV was playing loudly, but then it was turned off. In just a moment, she rounded the corner and he smiled at her appearance. Her headpiece was askew and her collar unbuttoned. The rest of her was covered in a long black robe. "Sorry," she said, as she felt his eyes on her face and veil. She looked relieved to see it was him standing there. "It's too hot to wear all this headgear. You don't mind if I take it off, do you?" She pulled it off and he noticed her mussed hair. She noticed that he noticed. "I have hat hair don't I?"

He laughed. "Just slightly. But you may want to go change clothes anyway. I'm here to paint!"

"Thank you, God!" she said, looking toward the ceiling. Then she laughed, a tinkling laughter that Clarence thought most beautiful. "I prayed for a painter, and here I have one! I'll be back in a jiffy!"

She went running down the hallway and Clarence stood in a trance. "Bad idea, Clarence, bad idea," he mumbled to himself. Was it too late to leave?

When she walked out a few minutes later in her paint-flecked overalls, he was glad he'd stayed. She was almost giddy with excitement that she had someone to help her paint. "These walls get awfully boring when I'm by myself painting," she said. "I wish we could have hired someone but it wasn't in the budget."

Her mood was contagious and the conversation was effortless, flowing smoothly with small talk - an innocent conversation, sharing bits and pieces of each other's past. The time flew by and before they knew it, they had completed the living room, with him promising he would come back in two days to do the trim work.

After Clarence left, Margaret took the paintbrushes to the kitchen and started running hot water in the sink to soak them. Her emotions were running amok and she felt a sense of shame. Why, I was practically flirting with him, she thought. "Lord, forgive me," she said aloud.

"There's nothing to forgive, my child." She jumped. Did she just hear God speaking to her? "You have served me well. Give into your heart." There it was again. She walked out of the kitchen to see if someone had slipped in and was talking. What did it mean? She shook her head to clear her thoughts and went back to her paintbrushes, running warm water over the silky fibers of the brush. She finally got them clean and put them on the dish drainer to dry.

"Hello", a voice called from the front. This time the voice was familiar. It was Father Thomas.

"I'm in the kitchen," she called back. He walked in. "I'm glad you're here, Father Thomas. I really need to talk to you."

"I had a feeling you might," he said. "Let's sit down at the kitchen table."

CHAPTER 15

COME SIT A SPELL

"Is it that time again?" Valerie had to laugh as Sam made a dramatic show of sighing, rolling his eyes, raising his shoulders and then letting them drop again. "It seems like it was only two days ago that the quilting bee met. I can't believe the week has rolled around again."

"Time does fly when you're having fun," she replied. "And besides, you don't have to lift a finger today since we left everything set up after our last meeting."

He perked up. "That was a good idea I had about leaving the chairs set up, wasn't it?"

She didn't have the heart to tell him it was her idea. If left to his own devices, he would have kept lugging the chairs back and forth from one room to the other on meeting day. But this week it would be different. Their picker from Connecticut was bringing a truckload of merchandise and they would have to use the quilting room to unload everything before they tagged, inventoried and put things out on the showroom floor.

Sam looked at his watch and scooted his heavy chair back from his desk. "It's 8:30," he said, standing up. "It's time to open the front door." He walked over to her desk and picked up some stamped envelopes from her desk top. "Are these ready to take to the post office?"

"Just one more," she said as she finished writing another check and stuffed it in an envelope. "That's it," she said. "Bills are paid for another month."

His eyes met hers with a worried expression. "Are we still holding our own?"

She smiled hoping to encourage him. "We actually have a few dollars left over this month. Word's got out that we're carrying a new line of vintage-inspired fabric. Lydia is even taking orders from all her friends in her old quilting club. Can you believe that we've made over $600 profit this month with just quilting supplies?"

"I guess it pays to diversify," he said. She smiled as she remembered those were the exact same words she had used when trying to convince him that they should open the back room as a quilting club meeting place. He took the last envelope from her as soon as she sealed it, and walked toward the front of the store with the keys in his hand. "I think I'll see if Luther Riggins can squeeze me in for a haircut while I'm out," he said. "Will you be okay here alone while I'm gone?"

"Of course," she said. "I've been here by myself dozens of times!"

"Maybe so, but keep the back door locked and ask before you let anyone in."

"I will. Go get your things done so you can be back before the girls get here." After a couple of minutes, she heard the front door open and then close. The entryway from the office to the showroom was open and at her vantage point it was easy to glance out to see when a customer came in. Most times they heard the old hinged front door squeak when it was opened from outside, but she had been after Sam to put a new bell on the door to announce the arrival of anyone coming in or out. He was getting hard of hearing and didn't always hear the squeak.

She glanced out and watched him as he paused and looked both ways before he crossed the street. He was still a good-looking man and she loved how his posture was still so ramrod straight. His military training had paid off. He never slumped like most men his age. She was lost in her own thoughts of Sam, and was startled when she heard a loud knock on the back door. She started to open it, but she remembered Sam's words.

"Who is it?" she asked.

"It's me, Valerie. I have a delivery for you." She recognized the voice of Ben Martin, the FedEx delivery driver. The antique store was one of his frequent stops. She opened the door and he stood there with a large box on a hand truck.

"Hmm," she said. "What has Sam ordered this time?"

He grinned. "This one's got your name on it," he said. "It's from an office supply store."

Her face lit up. "Oh goody," she said, "it's the new office chair I ordered for him. It's a surprise – he doesn't know I ordered it, and you picked the perfect time to deliver it. He's gone out for a haircut. I just hope I can get it unpacked and put together before he gets back."

"I'll help you," he offered. "I don't have a big load today. If it's like the other chairs I've seen from this company, it just comes in two pieces and the back is easy to slide down on the base. The worst part is getting it out of this cumbersome box. I'll go out to the truck and get my box cutter."

She waited until he got back, and he had the chair out of the box and put together in just a few minutes. He lifted the heavy old chair Sam had been using and put it in the corner where she pointed. "Thank you, Ben. I could have never put it together before he got back. Can I give you a tip?" she asked.

He blushed and smiled, his red hair accentuating the blush all the more. "No ma'am, but if you've got any of those chocolate chip cookies you make, I wouldn't mind having one."

She smiled back. He was such a polite and likeable young man. "I'll go you one better, Ben. I made a triple batch last night because I have a meeting here today. I'll bag you up enough to last you all day." As she put the cookies in a small brown paper bag, his eyes got wider. "You'll be in chocolate chip cookie heaven," she said, teasingly.

"Yes ma'am," he said. "I'll be running on a sugar rush the rest of the day."

"And Sam will be sitting in a comfy chair the rest of the day, so we're even." As soon as she got the words out of her mouth, she heard the front door open. "Goodness, if that's him, he got a fast haircut." She walked to the entryway and looked up front. "Oh, it is him, minus a haircut. Luther must have been too busy."

"I'll rush on out," Ben said. "It'll be more fun as a surprise if it's just the two of you." She started to protest, but he had already opened the back door. "I'll get this box out of the way for you, too."

"Oh, would you? Just put it out back and I'll break it down later and throw it in the dumpster."

"Valerie," Sam called as he walked toward the back of the store.

"Yes dear?" she said as she stepped out.

"I thought I heard voices. Is anyone here?" He sounded concerned.

"Just me and the ghosts of yesteryear," she said as he made his way into the office. "Sit down at your desk and we'll go over the things I need for you to do in here while we're quilting." She looked at him carefully. "And if you got a haircut, you need to go back and get a refund. I can't tell that he cut it at all."

He shook his head. "That crazy Luther! Sometimes I go in there and he's friendly and other times he's all in a snit. After waiting about ten minutes for him to tell me yea or nay for a haircut today, I just got up and left." Valerie watched as he pulled the office chair out from the desk and sat down without even realizing it was a new chair.

"Well I don't know.... Look at all these people in front of you." Sam was mimicking Luther and he dragged the words out in a slightly whiney voice as Luther often did. Valerie giggled. "And Valerie, there were just two people ahead of me and he was acting like the room was full. I told him I would come back later, but I'm thinking about going out to Fred's Barber Shop and let him cut it like most everybody else does now."

"Aw, Sam, give Luther another chance. He's getting a little older and doesn't cut hair quite as fast as he once did. We need to support our businesses on Main Street. What if he told his customers to go over to Lancaster to shop for antiques?"

"Oh, I guess you're right. I'll go back this afternoon. I'm just tired of his grumpy ways. It's like he's doing me a favor to let me walk into his barber shop, for heaven's sake." He sighed and leaned back in his chair. When his head hit the soft cushioned head support, it jerked back up and his eyes opened wide. He tried it one more time and had the same reaction. He looked at Valerie's chair to see if she had swapped with him. When he saw she hadn't, he put both hands down and gripped the leather arms, then turned his whole body around and looked at the chair. When he turned back around, Valerie saw the faintest of smiles and a questioning look in his eyes. Then he broke out in a full-blown grin. "Wow," he said, rubbing the pliant leather seat beneath him. "Just wow!" The look of love that passed between them needed no spoken words. Valerie's heart filled as she thought how much God had blessed their marriage. They had at one point almost given up on each other, but God had His own plans. Plans for them to grow old together.

CHAPTER 16

A GENTLE PROD

Holly McCarthy stood at the bathroom sink splashing water on her face. It was 5:45, almost time to wake Abby to get ready for preschool. It had been hard enough to get her own self out of bed. She'd thought about staying in bed and waking up Sonny, but he had worked late into the night, not coming to bed until almost 3 am. She examined her face as she stood at the sink. The dark circles had started about three weeks ago. Even Abby had teased her about them. She smiled at the innocence of her daughter when she caught her staring at her at the breakfast table one morning.

"Why are you putting eyeshadow under your eyes, Mommy?" she had asked. Then she had giggled. "Oh, I know why! You want to look like one of those old raccoons that Uncle goes hunting for, don't you?"

She had laughed with Abby and tickled her under her chin. She was fascinated with raccoons and had recently been gifted a stuffed toy raccoon by a family friend whom she called Uncle, although he was not her uncle at all.

"Yes ma'am," she had said, "a raccoon it will be. Maybe I'll be a kangaroo tomorrow - anything to make my sweet girl giggle." But on the inside, she wasn't laughing. She had tried so hard to learn to live without fear. She had tried to erase the images of her cancer-ridden body before her treatments just a year ago, and with the previous cancer before that. She unbuttoned her pajama top and took it off. There were still some faint scars, but the reconstruction surgery almost three years ago, on both breasts had been successful. What she hadn't known at the time was that just two years later she would be in a strange town battling brain cancer. Despite her fatigue and unsettled stomach, she smiled. So much had happened in the last year. Park Place was her home now, no longer a strange town.

"Mommy, I'm awake." Her daughter's sweet voice brought her alert and filled her heart with joy.

"You must have a built-in alarm clock, sweet girl," she said as she walked in Abby's bedroom and sat down on the edge of the bed. "And it's set for six o'clock every morning."

"It's not me, it's Basil," she said as the black cat who was pouncing on her daughter's nightstand leaped over her head and pounced on Abby. "I think we need to reset his clock, don't we Mommy?"

"Or keep him out of your room," Holly said.

Abby's eyes opened wide. "Oh no, he would be too lonely without me," she said.

Or more than likely the other way around, Holly thought. She remembered what it had been like being an only child, especially in her own case, being born to parents in their mid-forties who had thought they were past their childbearing years. She had always hoped Abby would someday have a brother or sister, but because of the type of chemotherapy she'd had, her chances of ever becoming pregnant were slim to none. And should she even want another baby? What if the cancer came back and she died?

She shook her head, mentally scolding herself. Enough of that! She started rummaging in Abby's drawers and found a pink shirt and black leggings for her to wear. Abby was still busy playing with the cat. "Go brush your teeth Abby and get dressed. I'll be getting your breakfast ready. And keep that cat away from your leggings or you'll look like a furry monster going to school." Abby giggled at the thought.

As she walked down the hall and to the kitchen, she searched her mind for the Bible verses she had memorized about being afraid. Isaiah 41:10 was the first thing that came to mind.

"So do not fear, for I am with you;
do not be dismayed, for I am your God.
I will strengthen you and help you;
I will uphold you with my righteous right hand."

She decided to claim it for her own today. If it didn't last, she had a whole list of them to fall back on. Maybe quilting with the other ladies would be a good distraction today. It would at least get her mind off the overwhelming fatigue.

***

"Ouch!" Holly put her needle aside and lifted her sore finger to her mouth. Looking at her quilting partner sheepishly, she half-smiled, but Valerie noticed that the smile was only a surface one. "I guess I should practice what I preach," she said. "There's a reason for wearing thimbles when you are hand-stitching." Valerie smiled in return as she tried to gauge the young woman's eyes.

Holly had not been herself all morning. Maura, her mother-in-law glanced over with a look of concern. She must have noticed it too, Valerie thought. The others in the room were chatting as they worked, but Holly had been unusually quiet.

"Are you feeling okay?" she asked. "You're not your usual bubbly self." Holly nodded but Valerie was shocked when she looked like she was about to cry. Oh, I've said too much, she thought, and then voiced her concern to Holly. "I'm sorry. I didn't mean to pry." She was dismayed when Holly burst into tears.

"Oh dear," she said, putting her sewing supplies aside and rubbing her hands together. "What have I said?"

Everyone in the room stopped what they were doing at the outburst. Maura rushed over and put her arms around her daughter-in-law and kept them there as Holly sobbed on her shoulder. The local ladies who knew Holly's story gathered around her, love and compassion written all over their faces. She finally got herself under control and Maura loosened her hold. Holly looked up at the women surrounding her who were clucking like mother hens.

"I'm sorry," she said. "I don't know what came over me. I'm not usually so emotional." It was true. Maura could attest to that. She had never seen her anything but cool and calm, even through her adversities.

"Are you feeling okay?" Jenny Braswell asked. "You're not hurting anywhere, are you?" She said what was on everyone's mind. It was all still fresh on their minds how Holly had come to be in town. The young woman was only in her twenties when she came to Park Place last year thinking she only had a short while to live. She brought her five-year old daughter with her, hoping to convince the parents of the child's father to take care of her after she passed away. Just before they reached Park Place, they were in a car accident which left Holly in a coma and little Abby not knowing why they had come. It was only through God's grace that everything had worked out the way it had.

Valerie remembered well the happy ending. Holly's surgery and subsequent treatment for the cancer was a success and when it was found that Maura's son, Sonny was the father of little Abby, they were reunited as a family. He hadn't known he was a father and was thrilled. It would have been so tragic if it hadn't turned out the way it had, Valerie thought. She looked at the young woman who had been through so much. She had every reason to be emotional, bitter even. Valerie shook away the thoughts and tuned back in to the people around her. Holly was talking.

"I don't really hurt anywhere. I just feel exhausted all the time and have vague symptoms like headaches, nausea and shakiness. The best word I can think of to describe it is 'blah' if you know what I mean. Not just plain blah, but super-blah", she said, laughing nervously. "It's hard to explain."

The kind faces around her were etched with worry lines and they were all wondering the same thing. Had her cancer come back so soon? The three of them who didn't know Holly so well had remained seated. Lydia, Kay and Sister Margaret were taking it all in and from the looks of concern seen round the room, they knew that it wasn't just a simple 'blah' matter. Margaret got up from her chair and went to kneel beside the young woman. "Holly, I don't know you that well, but I've heard you talk about your husband and young daughter. Could it be that you're expecting a baby?"

A look of surprise registered on all their faces and they looked at Holly expectantly. She shook her head. "I'm afraid the effects of so much chemo took care of that, she said. I saw Dr. Anderson about six months ago, and he gave me pretty much a zero chance of ever having more babies. In my heart, I already knew the answer because I'd done so much research on chemo and reproduction, but I had to ask him." She looked down at the floor. "Sonny and I have even considered adopting, but now...." She let the sentence trail off like rain dripping off a window pane.

"Does he know you haven't been feeling well?" Maura asked. She hadn't noticed any difference in her son's state of mind lately and he'd always worn his heart on his sleeve.

"No, I kept thinking it was a virus or something. My oncologist said my immune system could be weak for up to a year after my treatments."

Maura took hold of her hand. "Please tell Sonny, Holly. And please hurry to try to get in with your doctor. Your oncologist is in Charlotte, isn't she?" Holly nodded. "Promise me you'll make an appointment with her, or at least let her refer you to someone here in town. We have some good doctors and a wonderful hospital for a town as small as Park Place."

"I promise I will," she said. She turned to all the others. "I feel better after getting it off my mind. I know I shouldn't bottle things up inside and with your gentle prodding, Valerie, I blurted it all out." She touched Valerie's arm. "Thank you."

Valerie sighed with relief. "Oh, thank goodness you feel that way. I was so worried that I had overstepped my bounds."

Sister Margaret spoke up. "I still think you should go see this Dr. Anderson again. He can give you a good examination and rule some things out. Chemo can cause hormonal changes and hormonal changes can cause the symptoms you have. It would be a good place to start."

They all looked at the nun with approval. "You know," Valerie said to her, "if I didn't know you were a nun, I would think you were a nurse."

She smiled. "It comes with the package."

Her smile was contagious and Valerie thought she looked prettier than ever. She also noticed that she hadn't been wearing her habit lately. It must be hard to move around in that bulky thing, because she certainly looked pleased to be out of it.

CHAPTER 17

HAIL MARYS

Margaret had felt a tremendous amount of relief after her talk with Father Thomas. He was a kind and patient man, answering all her questions without being judgemental. Clarence Foster had followed up on his promise to come back and help her paint the trim work, a job that should have been completed in a couple of days but had stretched into almost a week, each of them enjoying the friendly banter that came natural in their conversations. He had talked about losing his wife, and about the beautiful life they had shared together. When he talked of his grandchildren, it was easy to see he loved them dearly. It was this conversation that prompted her to ask him his age and she was surprised that he was thirteen years older than she.

His conversations would drift to his church and the admiration he had for the pastor, and the genuine concern and love the members of the church had for one another. She could see that Clarence's faith was deep and for the first time since she'd joined the Catholic Church in her teens, she found herself thinking of her carefree days as a child, living with her grandparents and going to their gentle little protestant church in the farming community where they'd lived. Those had been good days and the church didn't have the stuffiness and formality that she had encountered when she'd first joined her step-father's church. Catholicism had intrigued her though, and it wasn't long before she'd embraced it fully.

She looked down at the set of rosary beads on her desk and picked them up, fingering them as she thought about their meaning. The prayers that compose the Rosary are arranged in sets of ten Hail Marys. She'd learned to use the rosary beads as an aid in saying the prayers in the proper order and to pray through Mary as an intercessor who prays to God on her behalf. She remembered the simple prayers in the church of her grandparents. They had prayed straight from the heart and directly to God through Jesus, His son. Didn't that make more sense? She hadn't mentioned any of this to Clarence. Maybe it was time to get a fresh perspective by talking to a pastor of the protestant faith. She didn't know one, but Clarence seemed to think highly of his own pastor. It was an odd name, he'd called him. Ah yes, Rev Rock. She should give him a call.

***

Reva walked into Rock's office and looked at him with confusion. "I didn't know you had a sister named Margaret," she said. "I've only heard you mention Lisa and Allison."

"Margaret? That's a new one on me," he said, laughing. "Maybe mom and dad have been keeping a secret from me all these years."

"Well, she's on the phone, and she said she was your sister, Margaret. Maybe she's just a nutcase and doesn't know who her family is. Do you want to talk to her?"

"Sure, you've got my curiosity up." He picked up the phone as Reva walked out of the room, pulling the door partially closed behind her. "Hello, this is Rock Clark. How can I help you?"

"Oh, Sister Margaret from St. Gabriel's. I've heard good things about you, and how well you've organized the new shelter." He listened as she played down her role in the start-up and was surprised when she asked if she could come by sometime to talk to him. Maybe they needed more money for the shelter. He could talk to the session.

"Sure, when would you like to come by? My schedule? I'm in the office until 4 pm each day except for Friday afternoons and Saturdays. That's when I work on my sermon." He paused as she asked if it would be okay to just drop in one day. "That'll be fine. Just call before you come to make sure I'm here." He looked through the door to see if Reva had been listening, but saw she was busy at her computer. He walked to the door and she looked up.

"My sister is a nun," he said, "and she's just up the street at the St. Gabriel's. She'll be calling sometime soon to make an appointment."

"A nun?" Then a look of realization came across her face. "Aw shaw," she said. "And me thinking there was a juicy bit of gossip to talk about in your family."

"There may well be, but I'm glad it doesn't involve a mystery sister. I'm not sure I could handle another one."

CHAPTER 18

A DEVIOUS MIND

The quilt had to be in the antique store. Where else could it be? The would-be thief hadn't meant to kill Horace, just to scare him into telling where the quilt was. Horace had walked in the shop with a large plastic bag in his hand and had come out the back without it. Was it in the bag? Did he leave it there?

Horace wouldn't say before, and he sure couldn't say now. The sickly old man had died with just the slightest amount of pressure on his neck. It was meant to be a scare tactic. Who knew he would die! And why had Horace stayed around town after he left the antique shop anyway? Maybe he left the quilt there accidentally and was going back for it. The plan had been to corner him in his hotel room and make him tell where the quilt was but he stayed in town, the crazy man. But it shouldn't have been surprising. Horace had made a mess of things all his life.

Watching the window display of the antique shop from Main Street had been fruitless. If they had the quilt, they should have been displaying it to sell. Maybe the owners didn't know it was worth six figures to the right collector.

Breaking in had not been successful either. Who would have thought those old locks couldn't be jimmied?

Patience - it was going to take patience.

***

Sam was in the Sweet Tea Quilting Bee room arranging chairs. Their picker from Connecticut had shown up the week before and he and Valerie had worked most of the weekend sorting and putting the antique and vintage items they purchased from him out on the floor. A rare grandfather clock had been part of the inventory, and it sold to a Charlotte decorator the next day after he polished it up. He was especially pleased with that sale. Valerie had done some research, taken some photos and emailed them to all the collectors and decorators she knew within a two-hundred mile radius. It was a rat race for a while with people driving from as far away as Asheville to see the clock. Valerie had set an exorbitant price and as they stampeded the place, they were all trying to bid higher for it. Valerie wouldn't hear of it though and let it go to the first one who arrived, Charlie Sutherland.

"I said first come, first served," she said, "and if we're to maintain our integrity in the antique market, we have to keep our word." She was indignant that the others tried to wheedle it away from Charlie. Sam smiled as he thought about it. She was right. They all respected her more because she handled it professionally, and when they found they couldn't get the clock, they started digging into the rest of the new inventory. It went out by the carloads and when they totaled up their one day sales, both their mouths dropped open. It was more than they had sold in any given month since they'd been open. The clock was the drawing card and they had all come with plenty of money. He snickered to himself at his next thought that they all went home with quite a few dollars less than they had when they arrived. Cars filled with beautiful merchandise, but pockets empty. They had been blessed to get such a good load. Valerie had already called the picker and told him to get busy again because she needed another load much like that one.

Valerie had brought a radio from home when Madge mentioned that it was quite soothing to quilt while listening to music. Sam had turned it on and was listening to a classical station as he worked. They'd had to use the quilting bee room for sorting the extra inventory, but now that most of it was sold or out on the showroom floor, he was having to rearrange chairs and quilting supplies that had been pushed into the back corner. Moreover, now that the ladies were bringing their sewing machines, there were tables to be set up. He had most of it done when he thought he heard the door open and close, but then again, maybe it was the sound of Haydn's Cello Concerto playing loudly and greatheartedly over the classical station. Oh, how he loved Haydn, the Austrian composer's work, especially the two concertos composed specifically for the cello. The ladies would be arriving in a half hour so he kept working for a few minutes longer before going to see if he had a customer. Most folks wanted to browse anyway without a shop owner hanging over their shoulders. When he finished, he walked out and looked around the large display floor, walking first to the furniture section, then up to the front where the primitive pottery collectibles were gathering dust on display shelves. The sun was shining brightly through the East-facing windows, highlighting the dust particles floating in the air. Someone could get lost in here, he thought, but finding no one, he conceded that hearing the door open must have been his imagination. He really did need to get a loud bell for the door. The one that the previous owners used had rusted and no longer worked.

It wasn't the first time he had heard strange noises in the century-old building. Valerie had run out to get her nails done and should be back any minute. It would be a good opportunity to go back to the office and sit in his new chair and snack on a few of the cookies she had baked for the quilters. He'd got a whiff of them this morning while she was stirring them on the stove and had been craving them ever since - peanut butter chocolate no-bakes, his favorite cookie ever, and if he didn't get some now, they would be gone as soon as those cookie-eating women arrived. He had cookies on his mind and almost crashed into the man who was searching through some boxes of merchandise they didn't have ready yet for the display floor.

Trying to keep his cool, he stopped and stood perfectly still, staring intently at the man who had straightened up when he saw Sam. It annoyed him to find someone rambling through their personal stuff.

"Who are you, and what are you doing in our private office?" he asked. It didn't seem to rattle the man any and it was then he realized it was the same person who had been in twice before looking for antique lures.

"I didn't see anyone out front, so I came back here looking for you," he said.

"We have a bell on the counter just for that express purpose," Sam said, still seething. "In case you hadn't noticed, there's a large sign beside it saying, 'Ring Bell for Service.' It's hard to miss."

"Well, I didn't see it," the man said defensively which infuriated Sam even further.

"And when you didn't find me, you just decided to snoop on your own?"

"I wasn't snooping. I just wanted to see if you had anything new."

"Well I can tell you right now, I don't, and I won't be getting any fishing lures anytime soon, so there'll be no need for you to stop by anymore. Just take your business down the road, please!"

"There's no use to get huffy about it," the man said. "I have just as much right as anyone else has to come into your shop."

"Let's just see how many rights you have," Sam said. He took his cell phone out of his pocket and hit his saved emergency contact. "I'm calling the police station right now. Chief Hamilton can come right down and read you your rights about trespassing in a private area. The sign is very obvious," he said, pointing to the sign above the door.

"Alright, I'm leaving," he said. "But you'd better be careful about who you run out of your shop. I have a way of getting even."

"Jess," Sam said, as if the voicemail that was speaking to him on the other end was really the police chief on the line. "Come over right now. I have a thief on my hands."

The man ran out the back door as if the place was on fire. Such a shame, Jess said when Sam got through to the police department a few minutes later. Officer Cliff

Jordan had been only thirty feet away from the front door of Banty Hen Antiques making his rounds when the incident happened but the man had disappeared without a trace by the time he got around back.

When Valerie returned with just a few minutes to spare before the ladies arrived, she found the shop full of policemen, or at least it seemed full to her since every available man on the police force was there, even if it was only two plus the new Columbo.

"What a way to start our quilting bee," she said, shooing them all in the back office. But it was too late. The ladies all arrived at the same time. They had seen the squad car out front and the buzz of activity inside and were naturally curious.

"Does this have anything to do with the recent murder in the alley?" Madge wanted to know.

"Did your store get robbed?" Lydia asked.

"I hope they didn't steal our quilting supplies," Jenny Braswell lamented. "I'm glad I took my bag home this time. Cutting out those quilt pieces was hard work."

Valerie laughed nervously, "Oh my goodness no, nothing like that."

Rebecca Hamilton chimed in, "It was probably just a jaywalker," she said. "My husband lurks around every corner trying to catch one." She looked at Valerie and winked. Valerie was glad to have the police chief's wife there to make light of the matter. Everyone seemed to loosen up and got down to the business of quilting. At the end of the two hours, most of the team pairs had pieced together about a third of their quilt pieces. Valerie and Holly were a little behind the others, because Valerie couldn't seem to keep her mind on the stitching. Holly seemed to sense her nervousness though and tried to pick up her slack.

"I'm sorry, Holly," she said quietly as they started packing things up. "I know I slowed you down."

"That's fine, Mrs. Owens," she said quietly. "It must have been disconcerting to come back in and find a police car out front. You'll catch up next time when your mind is on your work."

She was grateful for Holly's understanding. She seemed to be feeling better today. Should she ask? No, last time she asked, Holly broke down and cried.

Jess and Clarence had been out looking for the intruder, but had come back in once again to talk to Sam. They were just leaving when the meeting broke up. They were polite and made light conversation with the quilting bee members but didn't mention why they were there. They walked out the front door as the women were leaving. Valerie noticed that Jess stood outside on the sidewalk talking to Holly and Maura while Clarence talked to Sister Margaret. Rebecca hung around as the others left. "Are you okay, Valerie?" she asked. "Jess has shared with me all that's been happening. Everyone's just naturally curious. It's been kept out of the papers, so they don't know the part you two have played in the story."

"I know, Rebecca. It has been stressful. I'm glad our shop was kept out the newspaper story, but I won't feel comfortable until they've caught whoever killed poor Horace. Let's go back and ask Sam what's happened. I didn't have time to get any information from him before everyone came in. All I know is that someone was snooping around in our office."

"I've got to get back to the orphanage or I would. You two need a little time alone anyway to catch up on what transpired. I'll find out the details when Jess gets home this evening." She patted her friend on the back. "Y'all stay safe now. Please keep that back door locked."

"We did. Apparently, he came in the front door." She sighed. "You go on now, Rebecca. Get back to those kiddos. Maybe we'll just lock up and go on vacation."

"I think I'll join you," Rebecca said. "Jess thinks the town would fall apart if he left." She waved as she started out the door. "See you next week."

***

"I don't like it, Valerie. I don't like it at all." Sam was pacing back and forth across the floor of the office, fuming. "I think I need to get a gun."

"Sam! You'll do no such thing. You know I hate guns. With no more experience than you've had with a gun, you'd probably shoot your foot off."

"You forget I was in the army," he said indignantly.

"No, I remember. You spent most of your time in an office."

"I went through basic training, Valerie, and I hunted years ago with my brothers. I know how to shoot a gun."

"Oh Sam, I know you do, and let's don't argue. I'm sure the guy will never set foot in here again. Especially since you told him not to come back, and if he was anywhere nearby watching, he would have seen how quickly the patrol car got here."

Sam stopped pacing and calmed down. "You're right, Valerie. Cliff is still out searching for him. They've also called in a couple of sheriff's deputies to search on the outskirts of town. If he's anywhere around, they'll find him and take him back to the station. They're viewing him as a suspect, did you know that?"

"Heavens no, Sam! I mean really, maybe we should go on vacation."

"Vacation?"

"Never mind, but it is a nice thought."

CHAPTER 19

DUMB CROOKS

"Well, that was interesting. What do you think?" Clarence had shed his trench coat as soon as he walked out of The Banty Hen. It was an unseasonably hot day for end of March, much like the Florida weather he had left behind. He balled up the coat and threw it in the backseat, then got into the passenger seat of the patrol car. Jess didn't answer until he got in and turned the ignition and cranked up the air conditioning.

"I think we need to concentrate on finding this mystery man. Right now, we don't know if he's involved in the quilt caper or if he's just another nut, but I'm leaning toward thinking he's our main suspect at the moment."

Clarence laughed. "Maybe he's both. After so many years in this business, I've come to the conclusion that most criminals are nuts anyway. We could actually arrest him based on what Sam told us."

"I suppose so. He did threaten Sam when he said he had his ways of getting even. But we can't put him in jail until we find him, can we? Let's get back to the precinct and see if this Balbini fellow has left Maryland again. If we can get a photo of him, maybe Sam can identify him."

"Have you tried looking on Facebook? If he doesn't have a page, maybe his wife does and wives love putting up family photos."

Jess smiled in amusement. "That's not the first time someone's mentioned Facebook, but you sound like you're speaking from experience."

Clarence shook his head and sighed. "I am," he said. "I finally had to make Teresa delete every photo of me on her Facebook page while we were in Jacksonville. How could I work undercover when my face was plastered on social media for all the world to see? You wouldn't believe the criminals we've caught though by searching on Facebook. They do the stupidest things. We had one guy who was charged with armed robbery simply because he posed for a picture with the gun used in the robbery and the cash he took. They think their friends are the only ones who can see what they've posted, but more times than not, dumb crooks don't know how to change their privacy settings and anyone who clicks on their name can see everything they post."

"I'm not on Facebook, but Heather keeps me up-to-date on the small-time crooks around here. They've posted some pretty stupid stuff too. A house was recently broken into and they took a 51" TV, a laptop and an Xbox. We had a feeling who the thief was, and the next day he posted a photo of his dog and in the background piled in a corner was all the stuff he stole from the homeowner. Before he could take it down, Heather saved it and printed it out. He's in the county jail as we speak with no one to bail him out."

"I hope someone is feeding his dog."

"That's exactly what Heather said!" Jess exclaimed.

Clarence gave a wry smile. "We dog lovers think alike. Seriously though, technology can save us a lot of footsteps.

In your case, even if you had suspected the thief had taken the TV, Xbox and laptop, you would have had to get a search warrant and make a trip to his house. With the Facebook photo, you've got all the evidence given to you on a silver platter from the crook himself."

"Yeah," Jess said. "Times are a'changing and we've got to learn to change with them I suppose. By the way, I noticed that you were talking to Sister Margaret on the way out of The Banty Hen. I agree with you and Cliff. She is attractive."

"Tell me about it," Clarence said. "She's the first woman I've looked at since Teresa's been gone, but I'm pretty sure it's safe since she's a nun. It's odd though - I sensed that she's lonely in a way that only someone equally as lonely can sense. Does that make sense?"

"Well, there's a lot of 'senses' in that statement," Jess said, laughing. "I think I understand what you mean though. Sometimes lonely people have a way of seeking each other out. But I always thought priests and nuns were beyond that. I thought they found their solace in God alone."

"Me too, maybe I'm just imagining things. Even if there is a spark there, I wouldn't want to interfere in her relationship with God."

They were back at the police station. Jess turned to look at him. "Wow, you're serious, aren't you? That spark must have been a sizzling one."

Clarence blushed. "I can't explain it, Jess. Something just clicked. I'd think it was sinful to have these feelings if it just didn't feel so right." He shook his head, as if puzzled at it all. "I know, it's really dumb of me. I'll put it to rest right now."

Jess nodded. "Yep, it might be best for you to stay away from St. Gabriel's." He parked the patrol car in the space designated and marked '*Chief of Police*'. As they walked in the door, Heather met them with her purse and car keys in her hand. "I was watching out the window for you. I'm glad you're back."

"I'm sorry, Heather. You haven't had your lunch break yet and it's almost two o'clock," Jess said.

"That's okay. I brought a sandwich, but I'm going to take my break to go to the dog pound."

Jess smiled. "Taking the dogs your sandwich?"

She laughed. "No, I'm fostering a dog and they want me to pick it up before 3 o'clock." He looked at her quizzically. "You remember Buster, the dog who got the stupid crook busted for taking a photo of him with the stolen goods in the background?" Jess nodded. "They've got him at the pound and if I don't pick him up, he'll be euthanized tonight. My Brandy's gonna be so jealous, but I can't let him die."

Jess heard Clarence's sharp intake of breath behind him and turned around. Clarence's face looked stricken at the thought of the dog being euthanized. He turned back to Heather. "We were just talking about that case," he said, "and Clarence had just said he hoped the dog was being cared for."

"It's not going to be easy," Heather said. "My landlord wasn't too happy that I had a dog in the first place. I had to pay a huge deposit up front. I sure hope he doesn't find out about this one."

Clarence spoke up. "If you can't keep him because of your dog or the landlord, I'll take him in for a while," he said to Heather. She looked surprised.

"Do you know what kind of dog he is?" she asked.

"From the way you're grinning, he's probably a mean pit bull," Clarence said uneasily.

She laughed. "No, not that bad. But he weighs about 120 pounds - a huge black Labrador Retriever."

"A drooler with a capital D. I should have asked before I offered!"

"You're right, Columbo," she said, giggling. "You may just have yourself a dog."

Jess just shook his head. "You said it, Clarence. Dog lovers do think alike. I'm glad I'm not taking a big dog home with me."

"Never say never," Heather said. "The kids at the Children's Home would love him. I was just thinking about calling Rebecca and see if she needs a good therapy dog."

He looked panicked, but then smiled when he saw she was kidding. "You wouldn't dare. I'll make sure they never know about Buster."

CHAPTER 20

THE EXAMINING ROOM

Sonny McCarthy sat in the waiting room with his wife, Holly. Her appointment was with Dr. Anderson, one of three doctors in the OB/Gyn practice. He held her hand firmly in his as they waited to be called back. When Holly told him earlier in the week of her concern over the fatigue and other vague symptoms she'd been having, he panicked and wanted to call her oncologist right away, but she'd been adamant about seeing Dr. Anderson first. He was sick with worry and he knew she was too. Even though she had felt bad for a couple of weeks, she kept it to herself for fear of worrying him. He had been upset, telling her that he would worry more if he thought she was keeping things from him. There had been too many secrets between them over the years and he wanted to know everything, the good and the bad.

He had fallen in love with Holly during his senior year at Ohio State University. After graduation, he moved to California for a job in Silicon Valley fully intending to get established, let Holly finish school and come back to Ohio to marry her and take her back to California to live. Her father intervened though, not wanting his only child to move away, and each time Sonny called, her father would feign some excuse why Holly couldn't talk to him. Finally, her father told him that Holly had fallen in love with someone else and didn't want to see him again. He was heartbroken.

Meanwhile Holly had found out she was pregnant with his child and her father led her to believe that Sonny had left a message that he was moving on with his life without her. So much precious time had been wasted over her father's senseless lie, but he thanked God everyday that she and little Abby had come back into his life. He hadn't known about the cancer she had battled all alone during that time, but in the end, it was her second bout of cancer that brought them back together. She was devastated when she was diagnosed and had traveled from Ohio to Park Place to introduce Abby to the family she knew nothing about. It had all been one great big miracle in his way of thinking and he couldn't imagine why a loving God would heal her, then lead her down that path once again. As he reflected on why and if only, the door to the inner offices opened and a nurse stepped through the door. When she called Holly's name, they both stood up and started walking toward her.

"Can I come with her?" he asked.

"You're Mr. McCarthy?"

"Yes, Dan McCarthy."

"Oh, I remember you," she said. "I'm Kathy Williamson. We were in calculus class together in high school. You were the nerdy kid, but you don't look like a nerdy kid anymore. Sonny McCarthy, right?"

He laughed. "We all grow up," he said. "And yes, people around here still call me Sonny." He laughed. "I tried to grow out of the nickname too, but when I moved back home from California, I became Sonny again."

"Back to your question," she said. "You can come back in a little while, but first, we'll do the normal weighing in, urine sample, blood pressure prep, then Dr. Anderson will do a physical exam along with the pap smear. When he's done, I'll come out and get you so Dr. Anderson can talk to both of you when he comes back into the room. Is that okay with you?"

He looked at Holly and she nodded. He gave her hand one last squeeze. "I love you," he said as he turned her hand loose. She smiled and fluttered her fingers in the air in his direction.

"Love you too."

And with that, she and Kathy the nurse walked through the door and it closed with Sonny on the other side. No, it wasn't all right, he thought. He wanted to go through this with her. He wanted to watch the scales as she was weighed and concentrate on them so hard that he could wish a weight gain into being. He wanted to hold her hand and soothe away her worries while she was undergoing the exam, because he had not been there to comfort her during the the birth of their baby girl, nor through her illnesses. He sighed and walked over to sit in the same chair. He knew his feelings were based on fear, and yes, on guilt, for all the times he should have been there for her and wasn't.

***

Holly stepped onto the scale. One hundred-fifteen pounds, five pounds less than she'd weighed three months earlier at her oncology appointment. Her weight gain had been steady up until now. Her lowest point had been the ninety-seven pounds she weighed the day she was released from the hospital in August last summer. The oncologist had been thrilled at her progress and she and Sonny had shared a fist-bump when she tipped the scales that day at one-twenty. It was exactly what she weighed when she met Sonny at the university almost seven years ago.

The blood pressure cuff tightened as it built up pressure and then loosened as she sat silently taking in her surroundings. Instead of writing her statistics on a chart, Kathy was entering everything on a computer screen in front of her. "Your blood pressure is a little low," she said, but not enough to be worried about." She looked at Holly and smiled. "Better low than high." She stood up. "Let's get you in the examining room. You're here for a routine exam, aren't you? Any concerns?"

More than you can imagine, Holly thought, but didn't voice it out loud. "Just fatigue mostly," she said. "And it's time for a pap smear. I had cancer last year." She said it so matter-of-factly, it was in the same tone as if she'd said she'd had a cold last week.

Yes, I remember. You were in a coma last summer after a car accident, weren't you? I have nurse friends who work at the hospital who say that your recovery was truly a miracle. There were so many people praying for you."

Holly smiled. "And I still appreciate all those prayers."

Kathy picked up a small lidded cup and handed it to Holly. "We'll need a urine sample first. See that little door built into the wall? When you come out of the bathroom, leave the cup in there and walk on down to Room 3. I'll be in there shortly."

She trusted Dr. Anderson. He asked a lot of questions about her symptoms and she told him her concerns. He continued to chat with her throughout the exam, making her feel at ease.

"So how old is your daughter now?"

"She's not quite six. She missed the cutoff date last year but in the Fall, she'll start Kindergarten."

"Have you thought anymore about having other children?"

"We've talked about adoption since I can't have any more," she said. "I was an only child and it was a lonely life. But Abby will be fine if that doesn't happen. She gets so much attention from her grandparents and her cousins, I don't think she'll be lonely."

"I wouldn't rule it out," he said. "You never know what God's plans are for you." He took his gloves off. "Well now, little lady. I'll go out and you can get dressed, then we'll go over a few things. Kathy will go get your husband. She said he wants to be in here when I talk to you, and I think that's a good idea."

Holly groaned inwardly, wondering what he had seen that made him think Sonny should be present when he talked to her. Kathy walked out behind the doctor and she got dressed.

She was sitting on the edge of the examination table fully dressed when Kathy walked back in with Sonny. As soon as he walked over and hugged her, Dr. Anderson came into the room. He shook hands with Sonny and they made their introductions. "You can sit in the chair over here," he said, pointing to the blue leather arm chair in the corner.

"That's okay," Sonny said. "I'll stand here beside Holly."

"I've got a better idea," he said. "Let's go into my office. There's plenty of room in there and you'll be more comfortable."

Uh oh, Holly thought. It must be serious if he wants us to be comfortable. She smiled weakly at Sonny and he squeezed her hand. Dr. Anderson led them down the hall to an office with a small loveseat and two more chairs. Instead of sitting behind his desk, he pulled one of the chairs close to the loveseat where they sat. "First, are there any questions the two of you have for me?"

Sonny spoke up. "Just the obvious. She's losing weight and she's tired all the time." He looked at Holly, then back at the doctor. "I'll just go ahead and spell it out. We want to make sure the cancer hasn't returned and Holly wanted to start with you."

"When was the last time you saw the oncologist?" He looked at his notes. "Dr. Woods, isn't it? She's the best."

"It was in January," Holly said. "A little over three months ago. I'm not due to see her for another three months. She changed it to six month intervals between appointments instead of the three we had been doing."

"But if you don't see any reason for her fatigue, we'll try to get in earlier," Sonny said. "When will the results of the pap smear be in?"

"It takes a few days," Dr. Anderson said, "but from the exam, I didn't see anything suspicious looking."

They looked at each other and then back at the doctor. Holly was the first to speak. "Really!"

Sonny was more vocal. "Thank God," he said. "I think we've both been so concerned, we were expecting the worst."

"Of course, it's the test results that will rule it out, but honestly, I think your symptoms are caused by something else."

Sonny sighed. "Oh," he said. "Did we get prematurely optimistic?"

Dr. Anderson laughed gently. "No, I think you have every reason to be optimistic." He pulled his chair closer. "I've seen a lot of women in my years as an OB/Gyn and I've sometimes been accused as being abrupt without much of a bedside manner. The truth of the matter is it's been my only defense in keeping from getting too emotionally involved with my patients. But today I'm letting my hair down, so to speak." he reached up and rubbed his balding head. "Or at least what little bit I have left." They both looked at him expectantly, afraid to get their hopes up. "What I'm telling you is that I am absolutely thrilled that both the urine test and the examination confirm that you're pregnant, Holly."

"What!" They said it in unison, then Holly spoke up. "But, but...we didn't think it was possible".

"Neither did I when I saw you last year. The ultrasound we did showed that your left ovary had atrophied and the right one was showing signs of beginning to do the same. This surprises me as much as it does the two of you."

Sonny was grinning broadly, but when he saw tears running down Holly's cheek, he grew serious. "What is it, Honey? Why are you crying? This is wonderful news...

isn't it?" He turned to Dr. Anderson with a puzzled look on his face.

"That's what pregnant women do, Sonny," Dr. Anderson said. "They cry. Get used to it."

CHAPTER 21

NECTAR FOR THE SOUL

Valerie pulled out her favorite tea pitcher from the cabinet where she stored the serving platters she used for special occasions. At the last gathering, Maura had suggested that instead of Valerie always doing refreshments, they would take turns and today she would be bringing her famous banana bread. Valerie insisted she would continue to provide the drinks. A stretch of warm days had settled over Park Place and this was the warmest of them all. Some would want coffee but most would want iced tea, sweet of course.

The vintage pitcher wasn't antique nor was it considered valuable, but it was the graceful curves and the hand-painted butterflies on the outside of the glass that delighted her. It was a happy pitcher, she decided and she liked to surround herself with happy things. She had never collected things for their value, but only things that gave her visual and inner pleasure.

She had made the tea hot, fresh, and strong that morning. Now, as she poured it from the plastic container into the pitcher, it was the color of rich, transparent amber. Thirsty, she filled her own glass with ice cubes and poured some from the pitcher. She took a sip, her taste buds appreciating the sublime, sweet flavor. Ah, sweet tea, she thought, a Southerner's golden nectar. She balanced the bamboo tray that held the glasses in both hands and carried them over to the rolling serving cart, putting them on the bottom shelf. She set the pitcher and a platter on the top shelf, along with her Lenox Butterfly Meadow dessert plates and the dainty butterfly cocktail napkins she inherited from her mother. She then rolled the cart into the quilting room and looked at the pretty display with satisfaction. It's a shame I didn't live in the days of Victorian England, she thought, where I could have been waited upon by a hand-maid serving tea every day on inherited fine china at my afternoon tea parties. The thought made her smile. "Get back to the present Valerie," she said out loud. "You're perfectly happy in this place and time."

But then a short feeling of despair overcame her. She had been a little down lately. Holly's health had been weighing on her mind. Hopefully she had seen a doctor by now. And this thing with the unsolved murder. She wouldn't feel fully safe again until they caught the person responsible. It was time to call Jess again and see if they were any closer to solving the case. In the movies, crime solving never took this long!

She jumped when she heard the sound of the new chimes Sam had just installed on the front door. He had gone to the bank, and here she was alone. She peeked around the corner and was happy to see it was just Maura, with Holly right behind her. She walked out to meet them and was encouraged when Holly flashed her a big smile. Maybe it wasn't bad news at all, she thought. Oh, what a relief it would be if it was just a false alarm. She wouldn't ask. If Holly wanted to share with the group, she would do it without her prodding.

Sam walked in right behind them. "Oops," he said. "I almost stepped on your heels, Maura. I'm sorry!"

"That's okay," she said, laughing. "I didn't realize you were behind me and I stopped rather abruptly."

"Hmm," he said, sniffing in the air. "Let me guess.... Banana nut bread."

"A keen sense of smell," Maura said with surprise. "I have it sealed up tight in a Tupperware container and you can still smell it! I'm impressed."

Sam laughed. "I must admit that Valerie told me this morning what you were bringing. I was secretly hoping...."

She cut him off in mid-sentence. "You were hoping I would share," she said, and handed him a plastic container. "I made a loaf just for you to thank you for arranging and rearranging to meet our needs in here every week."

Valerie smiled as Sam took the bread from Maura. "Really? Just for me?" His eyes had opened wide.

"You'd have thought you handed him a golden egg," she said.

Maura laughed and Sam went marching back to the office with a silly grin on his face. "He'll head straight for the coffee pot," Valerie said. "He hasn't had breakfast yet." She turned to her friend. "Thanks Maura. You're always so thoughtful."

***

"It's a good thing you gave Sam his own loaf of banana bread," Valerie said as she and Maura stacked the dirty dishes on the small cart. "He would have cried otherwise when he saw that not a single crumb was left on the platter."

"They did seem to enjoy it, didn't they?"

"Enjoy it? They devoured it!" Valerie looked at the women as they gathered around the sewing machines. Some of them were using shears to cut the fabric and some were sewing. "It's still so confusing to me that we cut the fabric, sew the fabric, cut it again and sew it again! All those little blocks.... You have to have the patience of Job to sew, don't you?"

"Pretty much," Maura answered. "You have to pay attention to detail, but like everything else, the more you practice, the easier it is to do."

"I don't think I would have the patience to do it like serious quilters do, but it's fun working on something simple. The baby quilt was a good idea."

"Has it been worth your while to carry quilting supplies?" Maura asked.

"Yes, it's given our business a boost. People are coming from all the surrounding towns to buy our fabric."

"You were wise to stock the reproduction fabrics. So many people are nostalgic for the look of the quilts made by their mothers and grandmothers. The 1930's through the mid-century fabrics are my favorites. I'm just drawn to them and I know it's because they bring about such sweet memories of those nights spent with my grandmothers who were both quilters."

"I just got a request for some Civil War era fabric from Andrew Jackson State Park. When they have re-enactment events, they're going to start having volunteer quilters in the old cabin. They'll be displaying quilts and demonstrating how to do hand stitching. Laura, their ranger, asked if we would consider volunteering. I'll bring it up when we do our brief business meeting after our quilting session."

"That sounds like fun," Maura said.

"Well, off I go to take this cart back. Get on with your quilting!"

When Valerie returned, Holly was cutting some of the squares into triangular shapes. "The hospital nursery is going to look so cheerful with all these colorful designs," she said, her eyes twinkling. Valerie couldn't get over the change in her these last two weeks. Where her complexion had been sallow and dark circles surrounding her eyes, now she had a radiant glow about her.

"You're feeling a lot better, I see," she said.

Holly nodded. "I'll tell all of you about my doctor visit once the sewing machines quieten down." She reached over and caught Valerie's arm and smiled. "It was good news."

"Thank goodness," Valerie said. "That's all I need to know."

"No, you'll want to hear the nitty gritty," Holly said with a chuckle. "Trust me."

There was a buzz of conversation in the room a little louder than the sewing machines. Everyone was listening to Lydia as she shared stories about quilting superstitions. Her voice carried well and rang loud and clear with the girls all paying rapt attention.

"Did they really do that?" Mary Beth asked during one of her stories.

"Yes, and have you heard the superstition about the cat and the trampoline?" Lydia asked.

Sister Margaret laughed. "Sorry," she said. "The thoughts of cats and trampolines in the same story is just plain funny. I didn't know they had trampolines back then."

They all looked at the nun with interest. She had been revealing a side of her personality that was quite different from the day she first stepped foot in the shop. Instead of the quiet, shy woman in a head-to-toe habit, she was turning out to have a great sense of humor, and had even gone to wearing normal clothes. She was really quite attractive and younger than any of them had thought.

"This was a makeshift trampoline," Lydia said, laughing. "The unmarried girls would gather around the quilt holding each corner and sometimes in between. They would put the cat in the center, then bounce it up and down until the cat jumped out. Whoever the cat jumped on would be the first one to get married."

"Ouch," Jenny said, "I wouldn't want to have a cat jumping on me. They have sharp claws. And why be in such an all-fired hurry to get married. I wish I'd waited a few years myself." Good natured laughter filled the room.

Madge spoke up. "And have you heard the one about the Wandering Foot quilt pattern? This was a superstition when I was growing up. It was the custom for family members to make a quilt for their son or brother for his twenty-first birthday, but they would never make the Wandering Foot pattern for him because, according to the superstition, he would inherit not only the quilt, but a real wandering foot and would leave his hometown and move away. No one wanted their sons to move away, because even after they got married, they were expected to help their fathers on the farm."

"I've also heard it another way," Lydia said. "A wife would never let her husband sleep under a Wandering Foot quilt because it would make him prone to stray from his wedding vows."

Mary Beth shook her head. "Silly superstitions. Maybe it was just an excuse to account for their wandering men!"

"It was a pretty pattern though," Lydia continued. "And one of the easier ones to make, so after a while they re-named it the Turkey Track to keep their men from wandering about."

"I heard some really good ones when I would go with my mom to her quilting bee at church," Holly said. "There was a pattern called the Drunkard's Path back in the early 19th century. There were a lot of them made to be auctioned off as fundraisers for the temperance movement, but you wouldn't want your son sleeping under it or he would be apt to go the path of a drinking man. They renamed that one too. I've heard the pattern called *The Oregon Trail*. It's also called *Solomon's Puzzle*." When she finished talking, she noticed all the women were staring at her.

Mary Beth spoke up. "Holly, you look so much better than you did last week. Are you feeling better?"

Maura and Holly's eyes met. They were both smiling. "Yes, that's another thing I wanted to share with all of you today. I was just waiting for the right time."

"It must be good news or you wouldn't be smiling," Mary Beth said.

"It is. I don't have cancer."

"Thank God," they all said in unison.

"It's a miracle," Madge said. "We prayed your bad health and your symptoms away."

Holly looked at the octogenarian and smiled. Madge was such a spunky lady to be in her mid-eighties. Even now, when the others in the group were dressed in either jeans or comfy casual, Madge was, as always, dressed to the nines. A smart and obviously expensive white tunic was paired with crisp black linen pants. The necklace she wore was a simple long gold chain anchored with a slim gold giraffe pendant. Holly knew enough about jewelry to recognize it as fine, and not costume. Black patent-leather flats and her signature red lipstick completed the look. Her dark hair was cut in a pageboy - a great cut and color, Holly thought. Madge was looking at her expectantly.

"Bad health; yes you prayed it away, but not all my symptoms. The symptoms are still there, but not quite so bad. But of course, they're perfectly normal symptoms."

"Normal for what?" Valerie asked.

Holly paused. She looked around at the expectant faces and gave them a big smile. "Normal for someone who's going to have a baby!"

The room went silent for all of thirty seconds, then it exploded with voice over voice, each trying to outtalk the others. Where the quilting bee had ended on a solemn note a couple of weeks before, it was ending with joy and hugs all around this time.

CHAPTER 22

HEART SHAPES

Tuesday afternoon was always clean-up day in The Banty Hen. It had been after 12:30 when the quilting members had gone. They stayed longer than normal, talking and congratulating Holly. Valerie did have a chance to ask the others about volunteering at the State Park and three of them had committed. Sam was whistling as he whisked away the dust from the bookshelf full of Josef Originals figurines.

"I don't understand how everything gets so dusty," he said. "I have to wipe these shelves down twice a week."

"There will always be dust in these old buildings," Valerie said. "I think it filters down from the attic. There's years of it stored away up there." She had the glass cleaner out and was wiping down the top of the glass counter. The new door chimes rang and they both looked up at the same time and watched a middle-aged woman walk through the doors. Valerie thought there was something familiar about her and when she reached the counter and started speaking, Valerie knew who she was. It was the lady who had been so interested in antique quilts right before the murder happened.

"Just thought I would try one more time before I leave town," she said. "I hope you've taken some time to scout out some old quilts since I was in here last. Or maybe finally putting some out that you've had packed away."

Valerie took a moment before she replied, taking time to assess her feelings. What was it about this woman that made her so intensely dislike her? The person standing in front of her wasn't particularly pleasing to the eye, but she had never thought herself one to judge people on their looks. She was wearing a long flowing caftan. A pretty scarf was being used as a headband, pulling her salt and pepper hair sharply away from her forehead causing the heart-shaped birthmark to stand out even more. A leather crossbody purse with tassels was hanging from one shoulder. It would have been a chic look if it had been worn by anyone else, she thought. Maybe she was offended at the stranger's presumption of speaking with such a superior attitude. Get a grip, Valerie, she mentally reminded herself. She is the customer and you are the shop owner. Be nice!

"Oh, welcome back!" she said with as much enthusiasm as she could muster. "I hope you're doing well today?" The woman nodded curtly. She made Valerie nervous, and when she was nervous, she prattled and made small talk. "We haven't been on any buying trips lately, so I'm afraid our inventory hasn't changed much except for some nice furniture pieces and my new line of quilting supplies."

"Hmph, you don't have much of a shop here, do you?" Valerie was taken aback and didn't know what to say. Sam had listened to the exchange and quit his dusting and walked toward the counter.

"Is there a problem, Valerie?" he asked. The woman looked surprised at Sam's sudden appearance but made it a point not to look at him. It seemed to Valerie as if she didn't want him to get a good look at her.

"I don't know," Valerie said. "I think our customer was expecting our shop to be a little more than it is."

"No, no, I'm just disappointed," the woman said. "I'm sorry to have bothered you," and with that, she turned around and walked out the door.

"Good riddance," Sam said as the chime sounded when the door closed behind her. He turned and looked at his wife. "What was that all about? She's a strange and rude one, isn't she?"

"I hope she never comes back," Valerie said. "She makes me nervous."

"There's something so familiar about her," Sam said. "I know I've seen that face before and it's driving me crazy that I can't remember where."

"She's been in here before, I'm sure I told you about her. She's looking for antique quilts. And I, for one, am going to forget about her," she said. "I'm going to the back and fix your lunch. I brought the leftover chicken and dumplings we had for supper last night and all I have to do is warm them up in the microwave."

"Great, I love your chicken and dumplings!"

She laughed. "What don't you love?" she asked.

"Barking dogs and rude people like the one we just had in here," he answered.

A short while later, the aroma of chicken and dumplings was drifting out into the front of the shop. Sam put the duster away and walked to the back where Valerie had just spooned a generous portion onto his plate. "There's some sweet tea in the fridge," she said. "Pour both of us a glass if you don't mind." He poured the tea and handed Valerie hers. Just then the chime on the door sounded again.

She set the glass on the small table. "I'll go see who it is as soon as I finish filling my plate," Valerie said and spooned the remainder of the chicken and dumplings in her own plate. "Go ahead and start eating before it gets cold." She peeked around the corner and saw that her friend, Donna Clemmons and several other ladies had come in. She walked out just far enough for them to see her and waved. "Good afternoon, ladies," she said. "Donna, it's good to see you."

Donna took a few steps closer so she could hear her. "Hi Valerie, I brought our book club by to see what you have," she said. "The novel we're reading is based in an antique shop and it's piqued our interest in antiques, so we decided to come in and look around."

"Great! We're glad to have you." Her greeting was sincere. Valerie liked Donna. She and her attorney husband, Mason were active in the small town, doing all kinds of volunteer work for charitable organizations.

Donna sniffed the air. "I smell some mouth-watering food, so you go ahead and eat while we browse around."

"Okay," she said. "If you need anything, just let us know. We'll be out in a few minutes."

"Oh, we will."

Sam hadn't started eating yet and as soon as Valerie sat down, he said grace, blessing their food. As they ate, they talked and the subject of the woman came up again.

"We've had our share of strange customers lately," Valerie said.

"Yes, we have," Sam said. "First the antique fishing lure guy and now the crazy antique quilt lady. I must say they're both strange in very similar ways. I think it's their attitudes."

"And it all seemed to start after poor Horace was found dead in the alley," Valerie said. "It seems an odd coincidence."

"I hadn't thought about it, but that's exactly when it started. I wonder if the two of them have a connection. Especially since she's looking for an antique quilt. I'm going to speak to Jess this afternoon about it. He should've let the public know about the quilt and that it's being kept at the police station. If the murderer thinks it's still here, he or she is apt to come hunting it."

"Maybe they already have," Valerie said. "The man snooping around could be the murderer. I would feel much safer if they caught whoever it was."

"And I would feel much safer if word got out that we don't have the quilt here in the shop. You know, I just remembered that Jess asked us to call him if that woman came back to the shop. I'll call him as soon as I clean up." He scooped up the last remaining bit of his food from his plate and put it in his mouth, then guzzled the last of the tea. "And by the way, your chicken and dumplings are even better warmed over."

The front door chime sounded again. "Oh, the ladies must have left without saying goodbye," Valerie said. "I'll go see." When she walked into the shop, she saw them still there.

"We're still looking," Donna said. "You've got some nice things in here."

"Thanks, I thought I heard you leave. I'm glad you're still here."

"No, it was someone who walked in ahead of us. She held the door open for us, and then went off browsing on her own. The last I saw her, she was looking at that little side table near the back. Then she left in a hurry."

"What did she look like?" Valerie asked.

"Tall and slim and wearing one of those long, loose dresses that look so comfortable." She laughed. "But only on skinny people, not full-figured people like myself." Her laughter subsided when she saw the color had drained from Valerie's face. "Is something wrong, Valerie?" she asked.

Valerie was somewhat dazed, but shook her head. "It's just that this woman is becoming somewhat of a pest. She had been in here not ten minutes before you all came in. I didn't expect her back so soon."

"You know, I did think it rather odd the way she was acting. She was walking in the direction of the post office, but stopped when she saw the five of us walking this way. When we stopped outside your front door chatting before we came in, she turned around and rushed back. She stood at the door as if waiting for us to come in and when I reached for the door handle, she beat me to it and opened the door for us. She motioned us to go in ahead of her. Then she made a beeline for the back like she was on a mission, and like I said, she huddled around the little table near your office examining every inch of it."

"So, she was within hearing distance of any conversation Sam and I would have had while we were eating lunch?"

"I would think so. I could hear a mumble of your conversation from up here, but couldn't understand anything you were saying." She looked suddenly interested. "Do you think she's a spy from your competition?" When Valerie gave her a quizzical look, she laughed. "I'm sorry, I didn't mean to pry. I've been reading too many mystery books. This is what happens when a book club gets together."

Valerie relaxed and smiled, trying to downplay the incident. "Who knows, maybe she is an antique store owner, after all. I guess she didn't think we were too much competition since she hurried out so fast." She changed the subject. "Did you find any treasures that you can't go home without?" she asked teasingly.

"I think Connie found something," she said, pointing to the petite brunette holding a jadite Fire King mixing bowl in her hands. But most of us are doing what all antique store owners find irritating, I'm sure."

"What's that?" Valerie asked.

"Reminiscing and saying things like, 'this reminds me of my grandmother's house', or 'My Aunt Betsy always made her potato salad in a bowl like this'. Be honest, don't you hear things like that all the time?"

Valerie rolled her eyes and laughed. "All the time! But it's really kind of fun to hear our customers reminisce about days gone by. If it gives them pleasure, it gives me pleasure."

Donna's expression became serious. "You're a kind-hearted woman, Valerie. I can tell that something's not quite right about the woman who was in here. If she's harassing or stalking you, please let me know. Mason will be happy to write out a restraining order or something."

"Thanks Donna. I really appreciate that. She says she's visiting someone and will be leaving soon. I hope that's the case, but if not, I'll let you know."

"Please do." The other ladies in the book club had gathered at the counter. "It looks like we're ready to go," Donna said. "It seems some of the others have found treasures too." They walked to the counter together.

After she rang up their purchases and sent them on their way, she walked back to the office. "Sam, it's time to call Jess. That woman came back in with Donna and her friends, then slipped back here, right outside our door. She probably heard every word we said."

"I beat you to the punch," Sam said. "I just called him after it came to me why she looks familiar."

"Really, why?"

"She looks a lot like the mystery man looking for antique fishing lures...without the hair. He's always wearing a baseball cap, but there's a distinguishing feature they have in common - a heart-shaped birthmark right above the left eyebrow. They must be brother and sister. I don't know what they're up to, but it can't be good."

***

"Maybe they're one and the same," Jess said after Sam and Valerie filled him in on the strange customers.

"The snarky attitudes, the birthmark in just the same spot and the fact that they each have the same build and rather masculine tone in the voices."

Valerie visibly cringed as Clarence propped his feet upon a Chippendale table with tiny, delicate legs. Jess noticed and tapped Clarence's knee with his ballpoint pen. "Are you planning to buy that table?" When Clarence gave him a confused look, he pointed to the price tag. "$3000. That's what it'll cost you if it breaks." Clarence lifted his feet straight up in the air, carefully bypassing the table and lowered them to the floor.

"Sorry, I had no idea," he said.

Valerie smiled. His nickname was perfect, she thought. Their eyes met and he grinned sheepishly. "Do you mind if I call you Columbo?" she asked. "I know I've teased you about it before, but the name fits you so well."

He laughed. "A bumbling detective - guilty as charged. No, of course I don't mind. As they say, if the name fits, use it."

Sam's tone was more serious. "Jess, I do think you should get the news out that there was an antique quilt involved in the murder of Horace Gunther, and that we don't have the quilt in our shop. I can't help but think that Valerie and I are in danger, as long as the murderer thinks we may have it."

Jess rubbed his chin. "You're right. I'm beginning to question my judgment on keeping it quiet. I was hoping it would draw the potential thief out in the open and we could catch him...or her."

Valerie turned to him. "If you think the people are one and the same, which one is it, a man or a woman?"

"I'm tending to think it's a woman, Horace's cousin, because of the birthmark."

She shook her head in confusion.

"And we still don't know how the loan shark is involved. As a matter of fact, his wife reported him missing just yesterday."

"How does the birthmark come into play?" Sam asked.

Clarence shifted in his seat and turned to Jess. "Have you not told them about the birthmark?"

"No, I should have, but I had no idea the man Sam kept seeing had a birthmark too."

"I should have mentioned it," Sam said. "Somehow I missed the part about the birthmark with the crazy quilt lady until I saw it for myself today."

"I told Jess about it when he first questioned us, Sam," Valerie said.

"I guess it just went right over my head, Valerie. I should have been paying more attention. But even if they both do have a birthmark, how could it tie them to the crime?"

"That's what I should have told you." He paused. "Horace had a heart-shaped birthmark on his chest."

"Wow," Valerie said. That puts a whole new light on things, doesn't it? I'm more confused now than ever."

"It has been a confusing case for sure," Jess said. "Clarence and I are going back to the office. If she comes in again, please call me. In the meanwhile, I'm going to put out a press release saying we have the description of a suspect. It should make Channel 3's news tonight or in the morning and maybe we'll get some leads."

"Be sure to give both descriptions," Sam said, "in case she's dressed like a man again. I still find it hard to believe the fishing lure guy is a woman. He was so rough around the edges."

Valerie pushed her chair back from the table and stood up. "I can't believe this is happening," she said. "But, man or woman, this person is bad. Remember, she or he had no qualms about choking poor Mr. Gunther. Jess, don't forget to somehow get our shop out of the loop. I don't know how you plan to say it, but please let it be known that we don't have the quilt in our possession."

"We will, Valerie. Heather will word the press release. She's good at things like that."

"Tell her I said hello. She's such a sweet girl."

"Don't know what I'd do without her." He and Clarence both stood up at the same time.

"I'm glad I don't have to buy that fancy little table," Clarence said.

Valerie smiled. "Oh, come on now, you know you would love it."

Jess walked on out the door, but Clarence lagged behind, continuing his chat with Sam and Valerie.

***

Jess was in the squad car talking on his radio when Clarence opened the door and got in. "Okay, I'll see you back at the station when you've finished," he said and put the radio down.

"Now what?" he asked as he buckled his seatbelt. "I was convinced we were looking for the loan shark, but now it seems possible that our main suspect is Amelia Lineberger, Horace's cousin."

"But what about Arlo Bambini, the loan shark? Sounds like a Mafia name, doesn't it? I can just see it splashed all over the news with headlines like, *Mafia tied to murder in Park Place.*"

"Yikes," Jess said. "I'd just as soon pass on the Mafia headlines. It's bad enough that we've had a murder here. I don't know about Bambini. I really thought he was connected somehow, and now that he's missing, he seems more suspicious than ever. Who knows, maybe he's Amelia's long lost brother adopted at birth or something, and just happens to resemble her and have her very same birthmark and they're in this thing together." He laughed at how ridiculous it all sounded.

"Clarence laughed with him. "That's what I call a longshot," he said.

"Or the mutterings of a madman," Jess said. "And that is exactly what this case is driving me to."

They pulled into the parking lot of the police station and walked in. "We'll get Heather working on this right away," Jess said. He called out to her but she didn't answer.

"Where's Cliff?" Clarence asked.

"I called him while you were still talking to Sam and Valerie. He was at BJ's Diner eating lunch, but he should be back soon." He walked on back to the small area outside his own office where Heather usually sat. She wasn't there, but there was an overturned vase that just this morning had been filled with tulips from her mother's garden. Clarence had caught up with him.

"She must be getting some paper towels in the bathroom to clean up this mess," he said. "It's usually me who knocks things over – either my coffee or my tea about once a week. Let's go into my office while I call Annapolis. I'll have her work on the press release later." Clarence went in ahead of him.

"It looks like someone's been knocking things over in here too," he said, sounding alarmed.

Jess walked in behind him. "What in the world...?" Everything on his desk had been swept off and now lay scattered all over the floor. The drawers to his desk were wide open and the contents emptied. In a panic-stricken voice, he shouted, "Where's Heather?" At Clarence's stunned look, he shouted again. "Go check your office and the bathrooms. I'll check Cliff's office and the storage closet."

After a thorough check, they met each other in the hallway. "Downstairs," Jess yelled and started running down the stairs to the basement, taking two at a time. Clarence was right on his heels. When he reached the bottom, he stopped dead in his tracks, with Clarence bumping into him from behind. "Clarence," he shouted, even though Clarence was virtually standing on his heels. "Call an ambulance!" He handed him his cell phone. "It's programmed in my contacts as 'Emergency'. Tell them to hurry!"

CHAPTER 23

TALK TO THE NUN

Jess knew he would never forget the scene in front of him when he got to the bottom of the stairs. Heather lay crumpled up in a heap as he took the last step and turned to the right. He bent down and turned her head carefully to face his. That's when he noticed that on her left side, her silky blonde hair was soaked with blood. He pulled a handkerchief out of his pocket and found where the blood was coming from and applied pressure, holding it firmly in place. Her eyes were closed and her face was so pale. Jess trembled, afraid to take her pulse, but seeing that the blood was still flowing and warm, he knew she was alive.

It took the ambulance all of four minutes to reach the station, and Lonnie Welch came in the back entrance of the basement where Clarence stood holding the door open. Lonnie's face became almost as pale as Heather's when he saw her lying on the concrete basement floor. Heather was Park Place's only claim to fame. She had been a high school cheerleader, homecoming queen for two years running, Miss Lancaster County the year she graduated, and had been a finalist in the Miss South Carolina Beauty Pageant. Even more endearing was her sweet and unassuming nature, making her everyone's pride and joy.

Lonnie reached down and took her hand checking her pulse. A wave of relief flooded over him and his face regained some of its color. "A strong pulse," he said with an audible sigh. He lifted his head to the ceiling, "Thank you, Jesus," he said raising his arms to the sky.

"Amen!" The word came from Clarence and Jess at the same time.

Lonnie examined her head while Jess kept applying pressure. "That seems to be the only injury. Let me have a look." Jess took the makeshift bandage away and saw that the bleeding seemed to be under control. Lonnie put the cloth back in place and held it firmly. There's a lot of blood loss, but that's common with a scalp wound," he said. "She must have hit her head on the handrail on the way down, or if she fell far enough she could have hit it on this cement."

"Or someone could have hit her." Jess's statement came from a deep place in his heart and was almost a growl. Lonnie looked up quickly and was surprised to see the calm, easy going police chief showing such conflicting emotions. Relief and anger don't often go together he thought, but he didn't have time to ask any questions. With no response from her, he was sure she had a concussion, very possibly a bad one. He took the bandage away. The wound was no longer bleeding. He pulled a flashlight from his emergency bag, opened her right eye and directed the beam to the pupil. The pupil constricted somewhat but not as much as he would have liked to see. He knew that early intervention was crucial, so he did a quick check of her spine and limbs and after determining that there would be no harm in moving her, he and Jess lifted her onto the stretcher that Clarence had pulled out of the EMT van.

Cliff had made it back and was shocked at the scene that was unfolding in front of him. As they wheeled Heather outside, several onlookers had gathered as they were apt to do anytime the siren on the ambulance was heard in town. They watched at a respectful distance. Rev Rock had come quickly when someone called him, and as they lifted her in the van, he asked the other people there to hold hands and join him in prayer. His voice reverberated through the crowd and the ones standing there would later express what a heartfelt prayer it had been and the certainty they felt, after the prayer, that Heather would be okay.

"I'm going in the ambulance," Jess said. "Rev Rock, will you meet us there?"

"I'll call her parents," Cliff said. He was holding her cell phone in his hand and he smiled weakly. "I suppose it's the contact she has listed as 'Mom'."

"Don't alarm them," Rock said. "Reassure them and tell them to meet us at the hospital. They're members of our church. Heather's an only child and they'll freak out if they think she's in danger. I'll be waiting for them when they get there."

Clarence spoke to Jess as the ambulance door was closing. "Cliff and I will hold down the fort, Jess." Then he turned to Rock. "I'll call your secretary at church and tell her to get a prayer chain going, Rev Rock. "Her name's Rita, isn't it?"

"Thanks, Clarence. No, her name is Reva, and if you call her Rita, she'll give you a piece of her mind. And tell her I'll keep her posted."

Jess rolled down the passenger window of the van. "Clarence, I just thought of something. Check the evidence room and see if the locked cabinet inside has been tampered with. If not, there's a key ring taped to the underside of my bottom drawer on the right. Use it to open the cabinet and make sure the quilt is still inside. And another thing...." He looked around and noticed the people standing by were listening to his conversation so he lowered his voice. "I have a bad feeling about this. I don't think Heather's fall was an accident at all. Send Cliff out again, checking every hotel within a twenty-mile radius, giving them the descriptions of our two suspects. Somebody, somewhere has seen these two and the sooner we catch them the better."

"Okay, Jess. He and I will work together on it. I'll call the hotels ahead and I'll weed out what I can to hasten things up."

Lonnie turned on the siren and as they took off toward the hospital the crowd dispersed in all directions. Gathering from the conversation they had overheard, they now knew that there had possibly been a robbery at the police station of all places. And they knew that for some reason, there was a quilt involved. Whatever else was going on, they had no idea, but Chief Hamilton was sure keeping quiet about it.

***

"You must have misunderstood," Junie Crowder said when Larry Braswell brought the news into the Feed and Seed Store. "Who in their right mind would want to steal a quilt from a police station?" Cap Price, a frequent customer and member of the Monday Morning Men's Club was sitting in his usual spot halfway down Aisle 3, even though it wasn't Monday. He stood up and fluffed up the bag of chicken scratch he had been sitting on and piped in.

"Yeah, who would want a quilt this time of year, anyways? I told Madge this very mornin' that we need to put ours back in the closet 'til winter. I'm tired of being so dad-blamed hot all through the night."

"You men just won't do," Kathleen exclaimed as she walked in with a plate of cookies. "You don't know the value of quilts these days. Why I saw one at the auction the other night bring ninety dollars. But it would take a pretty dumb crook to steal one right under the nose of the police chief."

"But that's not the worst of it," Larry said, picking up a cookie off the plate Kathleen was passing around. "That sweet little Heather, you know, John and Martha Hill's daughter; she works down there and got hit over the head or something. They took her away in an ambulance. From what I could see, she looked bad."

When what Larry said sunk in, everyone got quiet. Then Cap spoke up, red in the face and wiping a tear away. "If somebody's hurt that girl, I Swanee, I'll punch him in the face myself." There was a collective sigh and an air of helplessness from the others in the store.

Kathleen put the cookies on the counter of the old store that had been run by her father before her. "Boys, many a' prayer has been lifted up through this old ceiling and I think now's the time for one more," she said. A nod of heads gave her the okay. "Lord, we know you're in the healing business. I'm proof of that with what you've done for my health over the years. All of us are here together asking you to wrap your arms around Heather and do what it takes to make her well. We love you Lord and offer this prayer in the name of Your Son, Jesus, who performed miracles of His own while here on earth. AMEN."

A chorus of *amens* was heard round the room.

***

When Lonnie rolled Heather into the emergency entrance door of the hospital, the hospital staff took over and she was immediately wheeled through the large double doors beside the check-in counter to the rooms beyond. The automatically locking doors closed and Jess was not allowed to go beyond that point. About ten minutes later, Heather's parents arrived and after pleading with the receptionist, Martha Hill was given permission to go back, but only with a nurse and with the understanding that she could only stay as long as the attending physician allowed.

Jess was glad to see Rev Rock walk through the doors just a few minutes after they arrived, because honestly, he couldn't think of anything to say to Heather's father that would ease his fears. He was too frightened himself. Rock Clark had such a calming way about him and he would help settle them both down. Rock had been the pastor of their church for a little over twenty-three years and it still surprised new visitors when they heard what the whole community called him. When the new preacher had come to Park Place right out of seminary, there had been another Reverend Clark in town, so to maintain a somewhat formal title to show respect, they called him Reverend Rock, which got shortened almost immediately to the less formal 'Rev Rock' which suited him perfectly.

Jess was right. In a matter of minutes, John Hill was talking calmly, and they didn't notice when Martha came out until she was standing right in front of them. Her husband saw her first and jumped up. "How is she?" he asked, once more anxious.

Jess could see the look of relief in her eyes. "She's awake but has a bad headache. They'll be taking her in a little while for an MRI to see what kind of damage there is. The doctor said, depending on the seriousness of the concussion she could be released later today or she may have to stay here overnight. They want to watch for any signs of swelling in the brain, and the scan should tell if there's a brain bleed. If she goes home, we'll take her to our house so we can watch her through the night."

"That won't be a problem," John said. "We'll take shifts watching her."

His wife smiled. "A good excuse to have her in our house again. I wish she'd move back home anyway instead of struggling to pay rent and utilities."

"Oh, she's fine, Martha. She wants to be out on her own. You've just had a hard time letting go of the apron strings."

"I know I have," she sighed. "She is talking coherently though, and that's a good sign, isn't it?" She was looking at Rev Rock as if he knew the answer.

"It sounds like a good sign to me," he said. "Who examined her?"

"Dr. Peter Braem was already here and he's a neurologist. I've heard he's good."

Rock nodded his head in agreement. "The best! He was Holly's doctor last year when she had the car accident. I'm sure it isn't by chance that he's on call just as it wasn't by chance with Holly. She would have died if he hadn't found out her other problems so promptly and treated her."

"I thought the name sounded familiar," she said.

"Did she say how it happened?" Jess asked.

She turned to him. "No, she had just woken up when I got in there and was groggy. I almost forgot, Jess. She wanted to talk to you before they take her upstairs and Dr. Braem said it's okay. Come on, I'll walk back with you."

"I guess I'm not invited," her husband said with a glum look on his face.

"Honey, she must think it's important what she has to say to Jess or she wouldn't have made the request."

"I know. Just tell her I love her," he said.

"I will. And she did ask you to go over to her house and feed her dogs, if that makes you feel better."

"That's our Heather," he said, "always worrying about animals. Of course, I'll feed them."

Jess followed behind Heather's mother as she rounded a corner that led to the emergency treatment rooms. When they stepped into the room, the only person in it was a nurse taking down some IV bags. "Oops, I must have the wrong room," Martha said.

"No, you have the right room but there's a change of plans. Your daughter's headache became more intense so Dr. Braem decided to go ahead and get her upstairs for the scan."

She put her hands up to her face. "Oh dear, I hope that's not a sign of something worse."

"I doubt it, Mrs. Hill. Dr. Braem just doesn't waste any time when he's dealing with head injuries. And by the way, is your name Jess?"

"No, my name's Martha. This is Jess. Jess Hamilton, the Chief of Police."

"Oh, yes. I know who you are, Chief Hamilton. When Heather said to tell Jess something, I never expected it to be the chief of police."

"She wanted you to tell me something?" Jess asked.

"Yes, I have no idea what she meant, but she said to tell you to 'talk to the nun'."

"What? Are you sure that's what she said?"

"Yeah, I wondered about that too, but that's exactly what she said."

He shook his head as if to clear it and mumbled, speaking more to himself than anyone else. "Talk to the nun? What would Sister Margaret have to do with this?"

The nurse gathered the IV bags and started to leave the room, but turned back. "Mrs. Hill, Heather will go straight to an observation room on the second floor when they finish her scan. You and the others in your family can go on up to the observation waiting room. It will be more comfortable." She stood at the door and waited until Martha Hill and Jess started making their way back to ER.

Martha walked back to where the others were sitting, but Jess stopped by the vending machines. As he scanned over the selection, his eyes automatically stopped when he saw the row of Butterfingers, Heather's favorite candy bar. He put a dollar in and pushed the button for number 9. A Butterfinger fell through the slot. He added another dollar and pushing the same number, another one fell. At the drink machine, he pushed a button for a soft drink, waited for it to fall, then headed back to the waiting room where the others were preparing to go upstairs. He handed the candy bar to Mrs. Hill. "Give this to Heather when she wakes up," he said. "Just looking at it will make her want to get well and eat it."

Heather's mother smiled. "I've found Butterfingers to be the only bribe that works," she said. "I'll dangle it in front of her." Her expression turned serious. "Thank you, Jess. You've been like a second father to our Heather. She loves her job and is always singing your praises. That was a very thoughtful thing to do."

"I wish I could make her well," he said, his voice cracking.

"Just pray for her," she said.

He nodded. Only Rock remained seated and sat quietly with a small pocket Bible open in his hand. Jess noticed that instead of reading, his head was bowed and it was comforting to know that Heather was being prayed for right this very minute. Since there seemed to be nothing else he could do, he walked outside. He had some thinking to do, but first he would call Clarence back at the office. He got his cell phone out but before he could call the number, his police radio beeped.

***

"You're not going to believe this."

"I would believe just about anything at this point," Jess said to Cliff who had just radioed him from a motel a few miles out of town.

"You'd better get over here, Jess. I'm at the Fairview Travel Lodge." Jess knew it well. It was one of the seedier motels in the county and he had received many calls over the years for everything from fist fights to drug trafficking. It was right on the North / South Carolina border and even though it was four miles away, it fell within the town limit. Regretfully, the rooms of the hotel were in South Carolina and the office was in North Carolina, which meant the incidents were usually his. The sheriff on the North side found it amusing, but occasionally the calls went in to him and he was gracious enough to take care of them.

"What's going on?" Jess mumbled, trying to swallow a big bite of Butterfinger he had just stuffed in his mouth.

"I stopped here on a hunch since I didn't have any luck at the nicer hotels."

"What did you find?"

"Just come on down here," Cliff said. "I've already called the coroner."

Jess spit out the mouthful of candy bar that he had tried to wash down with a swig of Coca-Cola.

"What the.... I'll be there in ten minutes." He was leaning against one of the columns supporting the drop off area of the emergency room, and at Cliff's words, he leaned back on it and banged his head a few times. He took another drink of the Coke, then threw the can and the rest of the candy bar in the trash container near the door. Rushing back inside, he told Rock he was going on a call, then flipped out his cell phone again to call Clarence. He wasn't at the station, so he called his cell phone. While he was waiting for Clarence to answer, he started searching the parking lot for his squad car. Clarence answered on the third ring.

"Clarence, meet me at the Fairview Travel Lodge in five minutes. When I find the car, I'll be on my way."

"I'm glad you called; I've been trying to call you."

"The reception is bad inside the hospital. I didn't hear it ring." He scanned the parking lot one more time. "Why can't I find the squad car? It should stand out like a sore thumb."

"You don't have a car," Clarence said. "You rode in the ambulance, remember. I'll pick you up in a few minutes. I'm gulping down a hotdog."

"Dadgumit, I forgot! Hurry. Apparently, we have another body on our hands."

"What the...."

"That's what I said."

In five minutes flat, the squad car pulled up to the Emergency Room entrance with its lights flashing and Jess hopped in on the passenger side. Clarence took off like a flash with ketchup from the hotdog stuck to his chin.

"I don't think I should be letting you drive, but it's too late now. The town hasn't authorized it yet."

"Aw - we'll be okay unless a cop pulls us over," he said, turning around and giving Jess his best Columbo grin.

Jess laughed. "Now that would be funny. By the way, why were you trying call me?"

"The quilt is gone from the basement, caput, nowhere to be seen. The key was on the floor."

Jess let out an exasperated sigh. "So, that tells us that Heather's fall was no accident. She was either pushed down the stairs or was hit in the head with something after being forced to hand the key over." He was seething inside. "Just wait until I get my hands on whoever did this. I'll...."

"You'll do nothing," Clarence reminded him. "And neither can I. There have been times I would have given anything to bash in a skull or two of someone we took into custody. Once or twice I thought it would be worth losing my job over, but in the end I knew fighting violence with violence wasn't the answer."

"You're right of course, but I can always daydream about it, can't I."

Clarence laughed. "Yeah, just sitting still and imagining that I'm pulling a criminal's teeth out one-by-one, or chopping a toe off with no anesthesia is all that's got me through some of the worst cases."

"You do have a sadistic streak in you, Clarence. Remind me never to get on your wrong side."

By the time each of them tried to imagine the scenario of pulling teeth out and chopping off toes, they were at the motel. Cliff was waiting for them.

"What's going on?" Jess asked.

"Plenty," he said. "When I got here and asked about the man and woman, tall and slim, masculine, etc., the manager said there were two people who fit those descriptions and one of them checked out about an hour ago, a woman. He also said the man and woman seemed to know each other."

"Maybe Sam was right," Jess said. "Maybe it's a brother and sister duo."

"I don't know," Cliff said. "Anyway, he said he thought the man was in his room. He hung a 'do not disturb' sign on his doorknob sometime after lunch today. I went to the room and knocked on the door so loud, even the dead could have heard me...or maybe not," he said with a slight frown. "I came back to the office and asked the manager to open the door. He gave me a little trouble at first, something about privacy, but I finally got him to open it. That's when I saw the body, slumped over in a chair. Come on, I'll show you."

The manager was fidgety and wringing his hands when Jess walked around him to get in the room. "Please...we don't need this kind of publicity", he pleaded.

"I'm afraid we don't have any control over that," Jess said. "Park Place doesn't need this kind of publicity either," he said under his breath to Cliff. "But you know, the news stations in Charlotte will be all over this when they hear about it."

"It's a shame they didn't go to a motel in Rock Hill," Cliff said. "Or at least across the state line. They could have gone fifty feet in the other direction and we wouldn't have to be dealing with this." The three of them walked on into the room.

"Has anything in the room been touched since you found him?" Clarence asked.

"No, I didn't even check for a pulse because it was obvious he was dead." He pointed to the bloodstained shirt the man was wearing. "See, there's where the bullet went in. He was shot in the back. The murderer must have used a silencer since no one owns up to hearing a gunshot."

"Or it could be they've grown accustomed to hearing gunshots since there's a hunt club right across the state line," Jess said. He looked around. The room had motel furniture that aged it to its beginnings. An old analog TV was perched on a 1970's Mediterranean-style dresser and a matching headboard was attached to the wall behind the unmade double-bed. Dingy brocade curtains hung at the double windows, one side pulled over to overlap the other for privacy purposes. A small round table was pushed against the curtain with a lone chair sitting beside it - the same chair where the man was now sitting, slumped over. The table held an ashtray with at least a dozen cigarette butts, a styrofoam coffee cup, and two whiskey bottles, both empty. A cheap nightstand with buffed out cigarette burns stood beside the unmade bed. Perched on top of it was a lamp with a stained white shade. He reached over and turned the switch. The stark, bright light of the lamp in the ill-lit room cast an eerie glow on everything it touched. A wallet had fallen to the floor between the bed and the night stand, so he reached over and picked it up. Inside, a photo on a Maryland driver's licence card stared him in the face. It was the same man, now slumped over in the chair of a cheap motel, Arlo Balbini.

"Any sign of the quilt?" Jess asked.

"Not that I could see without opening drawers, which I didn't."

"After the coroner takes the body away, check this room good and check the room the woman was staying in. I have a feeling you won't find it though. It's long gone by now. You have a fingerprint dusting kit in your squad car, don't you?"

"Yes, I'll get it."

Clarence was going around the room writing on a small notepad and Jess realized how lucky he was to have the detective working with him. He had much more experience in cases like this. "Clarence, do you mind staying here gathering evidence until the coroner comes? If you need any legwork done, Cliff can do it. I'm going over to the Catholic church and follow up on a lead. Before they took Heather up for a scan, she left a message for me."

"Really?" Cliff asked. "So, she's talking? What did she say?"

"Talk to the nun."

Cliff and Clarence looked up at the same time. "What?" They both said it in unison.

"That's what she said. She told the nurse to tell me to talk to the nun. I'm assuming she means Sister Margaret."

Clarence put his notepad in his shirt pocket. "Jess, I'll be glad to go with you."

"I think I should do this interview alone, Clarence. You may not be objective enough." Clarence's shoulders visibly slumped, and Cliff looked from one to the other in confusion. "Besides", Jess said. "I need you here. You're the expert at this kind of stuff. Also, would you call the South Carolina Highway Patrol and give them our suspect's description along with the kind of car she's driving?"

"Okay, I'll go call them now and then finish up here."

CHAPTER 24

THE PLEASURE OF A VISIT

Father Thomas had stopped the push mower and was mopping his brow with a handkerchief he pulled out of his pocket. When Jess walked up behind him, the priest had been so intent on mowing the lawn in front of the rectory, he jumped when Jess tapped him on the arm. "I didn't mean to startle you."

He looked at the fresh-mown grass, then turned back to the priest. He wasn't as old as he'd previously thought and he looked rather fit for a priest, not that he knew how fit a priest should look or anything. "That's a good acre you're mowing. Doesn't the church have someone to take care of the landscaping?"

The priest laughed. "They do, but he only comes once a month this time of the year. He's not scheduled until next week and the recent rain has made the grass grow like crazy. I want it to look good for the weekend services and I figured it wouldn't hurt me to get the exercise." He pulled off the straw hat he was wearing and shook it against his knee, then sneezed. "The tree pollen is getting to me. A fine yellow dust is covering everything, including my hat." His salt and pepper hair was slightly mussed from wearing a hat, and he turned to face Jess.

"I know you didn't come out here to help me mow the grass. Let's go sit on the porch a spell. I need a break anyway." He led Jess up the steps and pointed to a white porch rocker. "Have a seat," he said. He sat in the other rocker and took a long drink from a water bottle sitting on the table. "Tell me, Jess, how is the young woman who works for you? Our janitor said he heard she fell down some stairs. Have they determined if she has a concussion?"

"They were taking her upstairs for a scan when I left to go on another call. I suspect it is a concussion though, based on her symptoms. She was unconscious for quite a while."

A look of compassion came over the priest's face. "I trust she'll be okay. She's in good hands at our hospital. I haven't met him yet, but I've heard they have one of the best neurologists in the state."

"He is the best, and luckily he was at the hospital when the ambulance got there."

Father Thomas picked up the water bottle and started to take another drink, but set it back down. "Where are my manners? Can I get you something to drink? I'm not sure what we have in the fridge, but I know we have some bottled water."

Jess waved him off. "No, I'm fine, really. I keep a thermos in the squad car."

"Okay, then. Now, what do I owe the pleasure of your visit?" He gave him a wry grin. "Or did you come for confession?"

Jess smiled. "I really came to see the nun you have working here. Sister Margaret, isn't it?"

"Now that is strange," he said, his eyes twinkling. "Nun's don't generally have many men come to call."

Jess blushed, not realizing that the priest was joking. "Oh no, that's not it," he said. "I've come on police business."

"Is our nun in trouble?"

"Not that I know of." He knew he could trust the priest, so he explained the day's events to him, right down to his suspicion that Heather had been hit on the head and the murder of Arlo Balbini. "And Heather told the nurse to tell me to talk to the nun, so I'm here to do just that."

"Oh dear, I'm sorry to hear that! Two murders in Park Place in such a short time frame! Quite out of the ordinary."

"Yes, quite out of the ordinary," Jess said. "And about Sister Margaret...?"

"I'm afraid she's not here right now. She ran into Rock Hill to pick up some supplies for the shelter."

"She drove?"

Father Thomas looked confused. "Of course, how else would she get there?"

Jess blushed again. "I just didn't think, you know, that nuns could drive."

The priest laughed. "You've been watching too many old movies."

"Yeah, I suppose so," Jess said. "Sister Maria in the Sound of Music just picked up her satchel and walked away, didn't she?"

"Indeed, she did! Julie Andrews was quite a beautiful woman back then. Still is, I suppose, even though she must be in her late seventies by now."

"I was just saying something along the same lines a few weeks back. When I mentioned the movie, *The Sound of Music* starring Julie Andrews, my young deputy had never heard of the movie or the actress."

"I'm not surprised. It's more of a generational thing. And now, about Sister Margaret. Is there anything I can do to help?"

"Well yes, can you account for her whereabouts this morning?"

The priest took off his sunglasses and put them in his shirt pocket. "You're serious, aren't you?" Jess nodded. "Do you suspect her of anything?"

"No, but I can't leave any stone unturned. She's new in town, and my receptionist, lying in a hospital bed urged me to talk to her."

Father Thomas put his glasses back on and scratched his chin. "She did go out for about thirty-five minutes this morning, said something about an errand. I didn't ask for an explanation. She's a hard worker, that one. She's got this homeless shelter project so organized, I don't have to turn a hand. She deserves some time off."

"What was she driving this?"

"Her car."

"Is she driving her car now?"

"No, she's in the church van."

Jess looked around in the church parking lot but didn't see any cars. "Where is her car?" he asked.

"It's in our garage."

"Do you mind if I look?"

"I don't mind at all." He stood up. "We keep our mower and weedeater in there too." He led the way to the

garage and reached up to a keypad near the door frame.
After punching in a code, the door rolled open. A
nondescript gray Toyota was the only car parked inside. It
had been backed in.

Jess walked around the car, peering into the windows.
A small notepad was on the passenger seat, but otherwise
it was spotlessly clean. Wish I could keep my car that way,
he thought. He walked around to the back of the car and
stopped dead in his tracks. It had Maryland licence plates.
He looked at the priest who was close on his heels.
"Maryland?" he asked.

"Yes, that's where our diocese is - Baltimore. The car
doesn't belong to her, it's on loan to her from the
diocese."

Was it a coincidence? He wondered. He took a small
pad out of his pocket and wrote down the number of the
plates. "Do you mind if I wait and talk to her when she
gets back?"

"Sure, you can sit on the porch while I finish mowing
the grass."

"You go ahead and mow. I'll wait in the car. I've got a
few phone calls to make." As he walked back to the car,
his phone rang. It was Clarence.

"Hey Clarence, I'm glad you called. Any luck on
locating our suspect?"

"Apparently not. I haven't had any calls. I called
North Carolina's Highway Patrol too. They're checking
all the major roads out of Charlotte going north. I let
them know about the quilt too, in case she has it with
her."

"And the gun? Did you find out what calibre was used in the shooting?"

"From looking at the wound, I'm thinking a .38 calibre revolver. Balbini's wife has been notified of his death. That's the same calibre of gun he owned and it's gone. Maybe Amelia shot him with his own gun because there wasn't one found anywhere in either room. How about you, Jess. Have you talked to Margaret yet?"

"She's not here, but Father Thomas expects her back any minute. Did you know that nuns drive?"

"Do I know what?"

"That nuns drive. The car she's driving has Maryland tags." There was such a long pause on the other end that Jess thought he had lost the connection. "Are you still there, Clarence?"

"Yeah, I'm here. So, she's from Maryland. A total coincidence. You'll find that out when you talk to her. There's a logical explanation to what Heather said. Where was she this morning?"

"That's what I asked," Jess said. "But Father Thomas said she was only out for thirty-five minutes or so. She wouldn't have had time to knock Heather out, steal the quilt, murder the loan shark and take off in another car."

"I should say not! She's a genuinely good person, honest and sincere. We have our suspect anyway. We've just got to find her."

Jess laughed. "See, I knew it would be hard for you to be objective. I'm really just kidding you, Clarence. But you've got to admit, the fact that she's from Maryland and Heather asking us to talk to the nun; those things are enough to make me wonder if there's some kind of connection." He heard the sound of another vehicle pull into the parking lot of the rectory. He looked up just as the church van pulled past him and came to a stop close to the building. "She just drove up, Clarence. I'll let you know what I find out after I talk to her." He didn't wait for Clarence to answer and got out of the squad car just as Sister Margaret emerged from the van. She's not all that tall, he thought. He had only seen her once before and hadn't paid that much attention. She wasn't wearing a habit but a dress that fell just below her knees. She was pretty, but she didn't seem to realize it.

Waving cheerily at him, she walked to the back door of the church van and opened it. He walked up beside her. The back was filled with paper products and cases of bottled water. "Can I help you with some of that?" he asked.

"Sure", she said. "It goes in the shelter. I can get the paper goods, but carrying those cases of water kills my back." She stood back as he picked up a case of water. "You're Jess Hamilton, aren't you?" He nodded. "I take quilting classes with Rebecca."

He was surprised. "Really? She didn't tell me, but that's not unusual. She's so busy with the orphanage, we barely have time to talk anymore, but come to think of it, I do remember seeing you in the antique shop a few days ago, but I didn't make the connection. You were talking to Clarence, my detective." It was her turn to blush and Jess found himself wondering if she had felt the same spark for Clarence that he had for her.

"Did Heather tell you I came by today?" He didn't have a good grip on the water case and at her question, he almost dropped it. He set it back down in the van and got a better grip. What other surprises did she have in store?

He didn't know what to say. "Um, no. I haven't had a chance to talk to her. She's in the hospital with a concussion." Over time, he'd developed a gift of reading body language and facial expressions and he could tell her surprise was genuine.

"What! I was just at the police department earlier today and she was fine. What happened?"

"I came out here hoping you could tell me, since she left a message for me to talk to you." He looked at her wide, innocent eyes. "But I can tell you're as much in the dark as I am." He paused, wondering how much to tell her, but then forged on. "When I got back into the station this afternoon, she was unconscious, lying on the basement floor...." He found himself getting emotional and took a deep breath. "The only words she spoke in the hospital were, 'talk to the nun', so that's why I'm here." He looked at her expectantly.

Her eyes were wide open and a scattering of freckles across the bridge of her nose stood out against her fair skin. Her right hand was pressed hard against her chin and covered her mouth. "Oh my!" She took her hand away from her mouth for a moment, then put it back up and started chewing on the side of her finger and knuckle, a habit that Jess recognized as nervousness as he had seen it in other people.

"Did you see anyone come in while you were there? Someone who looked suspicious?"

"No, not a soul came in while I was there. Or at least I don't think so. I thought I heard a noise and told Heather, but she said the station is an old building and full of squeaks and groans. I went there to see you. When I told her what it was about, she said I should come back when you were there. She seemed to think it was important that I talk to you about it."

"I'm listening," he said, and put the case of water back in the van. Was he wasting his time? Maybe Heather thought the Sister saw someone enter the building when she left and could identify them. Oh, well, it wouldn't hurt to talk to her. She had come to the station specifically to see him. What kind of trouble could a nun be in anyway?

"Let's go sit on the porch", she said. "Do you have a few minutes? It's a rather long story."

"I can't stay too long. I have another situation I need to get back too, but I can spare a few minutes." He grabbed the water again and they headed for the porch.

CHAPTER 25

THE REST OF THE STORY

Margaret had grabbed two water bottles from the case that Jess put on the porch and handed him one. "Make yourself comfortable," she said, pointing at a rocker. "I'll try to abbreviate it since you don't have much time, but I do need to start from the beginning."

He nodded.

"I was an only child and never got to meet my father. He died in Vietnam just days after I was born."

"Such a senseless war," Jess said and shook his head. "I'm sorry."

"My mother and I lived with my grandparents, my dad's parents, in Maryland on a small farm for several years after my dad died. I was especially close to my grandfather, but when I was ten, we moved away and a year later, my mother remarried."

Jess nodded. He didn't know where the story was leading, but he didn't interrupt. She seemed to sense his restlessness.

"I'm boring you with this," she said. "I promise it will make sense soon."

"No, no, go ahead. Details are important."

She laughed. "Well, I'm the queen of details. Ask Father Thomas."

He smiled. "He's already told me you're getting him organized."

206 | The Sweet Tea Quilting Bee

"I can imagine what he said." She laughed. "He doesn't know what to think of me. I've been told I'm not the typical nun. No one's ever quite known what to do about me." She paused and looked down at her fingernails which were trimmed neatly. "Sometimes, I don't know what to do about myself," she said wistfully. She looked back up. "Sorry, I didn't mean to throw that in there. Anyway, when I asked for this assignment, the diocese seemed relieved to be sending me off to some far-away Southern town. But, I'm rambling now, back to the story."

Jess smiled and waited for her to continue.

"The move wasn't so bad as I thought it would be and Mom made sure I got to spend summers with my grandparents. She wouldn't go with me and I always felt there was an undercurrent of bad feelings between them. But later I learned the undercurrent was not between my mother and my grandparents; it was with my Uncle Al, my father's only brother. He and his wife were jealous of the attention my grandfather gave me. They had no children and my grandfather made it clear that I would inherit the farm and some of their more valuable possessions. His wife especially didn't like me and I tried to avoid her anytime they visited while I was there. She always belittled me to my grandparents. I know now that it was because of the one item that she coveted over everything else and was furious because I was in line to inherit it. And she wanted it bad enough to steal it."

The police radio on Jess's belt beeped twice. "I'm sorry for the interruption," he said. "It's my deputy." She nodded and he clicked the radio on silence and put it up to his ear.

"Yes Cliff, whatcha got? Really? Where? Okay, I'll be right there." He put the radio back in its holster. "I'm sorry, Sister Margaret."

"Please, just call me Margaret. Or Maggie. I was named after my grandmother."

"I'll come back later so we can finish our conversation. You've hooked me with your last comment before the radio went off."

She smiled, but Jess sensed that it was only a surface smile. "Please do," she said, "I think it's important."

He hesitated. Maybe he should stay and let her finish the story. But no, Cliff said the North Carolina Highway Patrol had their suspect in custody. He needed to get back to the station. And why, he wondered, had Sister Margaret asked him to call her by her given name instead of Sister? And what about Father Thomas out mowing the grass? Was there really a less formal pattern going on in the Catholic Church now? Or maybe it was normal; after all, he didn't know much about the Catholic policies. Okay, Maggie, Margaret, whatever her name was, she was a few years his junior, but he still felt it was disrespectful calling a nun anything other than Sister.

"I look forward to finishing our talk, Sister. I'll be back." She nodded and waved as he walked away.

CHAPTER 26
BLUE-LIGHT SPECIAL

Jess pulled around to the front of the police station instead of the back. He parked in a space reserved for visitors and got out of the squad car. As he reached the front steps, he noticed the azaleas were in full bloom. Heather had bought the plants at Wilson's Nursery when she began working at the station. That had been four years ago - it was hard to believe.

"The place needs sprucing up," she had said, when she opened her trunk and lifted them out one-by-one. "I even brought my dad's shovels."

Jess smiled as he remembered Cliff's expression when she handed him a shovel. "And you two are going to plant them," she said matter of factly as she handed Jess the other one. "Yes ma'am", they both had said in unison. Neither of them could resist her charm and her sweet nature.

He walked by her desk on the way to his. There was a lone tulip wilting away across some papers where just this morning the vase had held a whole bundle of them. His temper started to flare again just thinking about someone hurting Heather. She wouldn't even kill a spider, for heaven's sake. She would scoop the spider up with a duster and carry him outside, not realizing he would probably come right back in the next time a door or window was opened.

Cliff and Clarence were already in his office when he walked in. He strode to the chair behind his desk and sat down. "First things first. Has anyone heard from Heather?" he asked.

"I was at the hospital waiting to see her when Clarence called me," Cliff said. "They won't let but one person at a time go in."

"So, you haven't been able to talk to her yet to find out what happened?"

Cliff and Clarence exchanged glances. "Only what her mother came out and told me; that someone forced her to the basement to look for the quilt. Heather's mom was more worried about her condition than about finding out who was responsible. All she told her mother was that a man was involved."

"Really? So, it was presumably Balbino, our dead man. And now they have the woman in custody? Tell me what you know."

Clarence spoke up. "Thanks to the keen observation of a young rookie patrolman, Amelia Reinhart's car was spotted in North Carolina traveling north on I-85 right outside of Lexington. He blue-lighted her and she exited off the interstate as if she was going to stop. He ran the plates and as soon as he got out of the car, she took off. Just when he thought he'd lost her, he circled back around and went through the parking lot of an Arby's restaurant. He spotted the car, but she wasn't in it. By that time, more patrolmen had come in to help with the manhunt. It turns out she was hiding in the men's restroom of the restaurant. She even had a man's pair of boots on to throw them off."

"They probably belonged to the poor loan shark that she stiffed," Cliff said.

Clarence shook his head and laughed. "Look at us. We're beginning to sound like we're straight out of a cheap detective novel. Blue-lighting a suspect, manhunts, stiffing loan sharks and women hiding in the stall of a men's restroom; you can't just make this stuff up." The others laughed with him.

"What do you think happened, Jess?" Cliff asked.

"My theory is that Balbini came to the police station, hit Heather over the head after he got the key, stole the quilt and took it back to the hotel. Here's where it gets tricky. Maybe Balbini intended to run off with the quilt without telling his accomplice, and she killed him, taking it for herself."

"That's along the lines of what I was thinking," Clarence said. "It's about the only thing that makes sense."

"I'm going to call SLED in Columbia," Jess said. "With her being a suspect now in two murders, Horace's and Balbini's, it's getting too big for us to handle."

"I'm not familiar with South Carolina's terminology yet. What is SLED?" Clarence asked.

"I keep forgetting you're an implant," Jess said, grinning. "It's the South Carolina Law Enforcement Division."

Clarence grinned back. "Like I'm sure you would immediately know what FDLE stands for. It's the Florida equivalent of your SLED."

"You've got me there," Jess said.

"Anyway, that's why I called you. I knew I didn't have the authority to ask North Carolina to make the arrest since the crime was committed here in South Carolina. They're holding her until they hear from you."

"I'll call them first, then I'll call SLED. You got the number?"

"It's written on the phone book. That's the only thing I could find to write on at the time since we haven't had time to pick things up in here yet."

Jess looked around. The desk drawers were closed but there were still papers scattered all over the floor. "I'll deal with this mess later." He picked up the phone to dial the number. "First to get her arrested, then we'll have to wait to see if she waives extradition once she's arrested."

He looked relieved when he finished his phone calls. "SLED will send an officer from the Sheriff's Department to pick her up since all we've got is a holding cell here at the station. I was worried that I would have to go get her."

"That's good news," Clarence said. "Are they taking over the case?"

"No, the agent said they would send someone out next week but in the meanwhile, we're to continue our investigation."

"For things to have moved so slowly in the beginning, they're speeding out of control right now," Cliff said. "It's a little overwhelming and you still haven't told us why Heather wanted you to talk to the nun."

"Margaret," Clarence corrected him.

"That's because I still don't know exactly," Jess said. "After a short conversation about her childhood and her family, it seemed like we were finally getting somewhere when I got your call."

"Do you think she has anything to do with this case?" Cliff asked.

Clarence interjected, "No, she doesn't!" He said it so forcefully, both Jess and Cliff were taken aback. When he saw their reaction, he apologized. "I'm sorry, I didn't mean to be snappy."

Jess had been surprised by Clarence's outburst. It seemed Clarence may be harboring a bigger crush than he thought on Sister Margaret, or Maggie as she'd said to call her.

He got up from his desk. "Don't get your dander up, Clarence. I don't think so either. I'm going over to St. Gabriel's and finish my conversation with her right now. Cliff, I'd like for you to go back to the hospital and see if you can get in to see Heather. Use your badge. Tell them it's a law enforcement emergency or something."

"Maybe I could go with you to St. Gabriel's," Clarence said hopefully.

Jess stood there quietly. Clarence got the message without Jess having to say anything. "Never mind," he said. "I think I'll stay here and answer the phone."

"That's a good idea," Jess said. He looked at his watch. "It's 3:45. If I'm not back by 5:30, lock the station and go on home. I'll give you a call later."

The door to the rectory-turned-homeless-shelter was open letting the warm Spring breeze inside to clear the air of the paint fumes. Walking into the foyer and then the living room, Jess looked around and wondered who had been doing all the inside work. A lot of thought had gone into choosing the seafoam blue paint color - neither blue nor green, but a gentle combination. It was a soothing and restful color. As he looked around the large room, he could see how welcoming it would be to people down on their luck. The framed art pieces on the walls were lively and fun and looked like they had been created by children. There was a large screen TV in one corner with a cozy seating area arranged nearby. Scattered throughout the room were small tables with chess sets and checker boards. A leather sofa, loveseat and matching chair were grouped together near the fireplace with soft lamps gracing the end tables beside them. A corner bookcase was full of leather-bound books and paperbacks, all tastefully arranged. This wasn't an ordinary homeless shelter with make-do furniture and industrial tables and chairs; it was a setting worthy of inviting the most distinguished of guests. He thought of the scripture from Matthew 25:40 that said, *The King will reply, 'Truly I tell you, whatever you did for one of the least of these brothers and sisters of mine, you did for me'*.

There was no one in sight, so he made his way into the next room, a formal dining room. Here again, the room was spotlessly clean with a silverplated tea set gracing the long marble top buffet spread out along one wall of the room. The table was set with six place settings of fine china and looked as if someone was expecting friends and family to arrive at any moment. He was beginning to understand Clarence's opinion of Sister Margaret. It was obvious with the thought and care she had so lovingly put into making this a special place for the poor and homeless, she couldn't be involved in anything underhanded.

"Anyone here?" His voice was loud in the empty room. When no one answered, he continued his path through the rest of the old home. He heard music from another room and followed the sound. It wasn't coming from the kitchen, which was to the right of the dining room, so he turned left down the long hallway. The first room he came to was a bedroom holding two sets of bunk beds with matching colorful spreads and curtains. Cheery, he thought; a nice room for a family of four. The music grew louder and as he reached the next room, he paused and looked in. A radio was tuned to a country music station and there was Sister Margaret, putting new sheets on the bed and singing along with Carrie Underwood's song, *Jesus, Take the Wheel*. She and Carrie were both singing, but only Carrie was singing in tune.

"Jesus take the wheel
Take it from my hands
Cause I can't do this on my own
I'm letting go
So give me one more chance
Save me from this road I'm on.
Jesus take the wheel."

He listened in amusement as her slightly off key notes filled the air with abandon. She seemed so innocent and naive - almost like a little girl. She sensed his presence and turned around with a startled expression. As she saw his smile, she smiled in return, but he noticed she was blushing. "My biggest vice," she said, "is country music".

"If that's your biggest vice," he said, "you've got nothing to worry about."

She tucked the last corner of the fitted sheet under the mattress. "I'm sorry you had to suffer through my singing. I've always said that when I get to Heaven, God is going to give me the voice of an angel, because He gave me the voice of a goat down here." She turned off the radio. "I'm glad to see you made it back. Let me finish making this bed, and we'll go out to the porch. It's too nice to be shut up inside."

"Looks like you've been shut up inside a lot fixing this place up. It looks great! Here, let me give you a hand."

She handed him two pillowcases. "Okay, see if you can stuff these oversize pillows in these tiny little cases. Seems like pillows keep getting bigger and pillowcases get smaller."

"That's what Rebecca says. The orphanage has forty-two beds, not counting ours. They're set up much like these. Most rooms have two sets of bunk beds, except for the rooms housing the teenagers. They have just two beds to a room."

"That's impressive. I'm sure it takes quite a while to make all those beds."

"It would, but we never have that many children at the same time. Right now, we have twenty-three. They make their own beds each day, or at least attempt it. When the smaller ones need help, the bigger kids don't seem to mind helping them out. It gives them a sense of responsibility. The sheets are changed once a week unless there's an accident."

"I imagine it's hard on the children to be shifted from one home to another."

"It is. It's a heartbreaking job sometimes, but it's Rebecca's gift and she's good at it."

"Thanks," she said as he fluffed the pillows and put them atop the newly made bed. "We can go back to the porch now. I just made a fresh batch of sweet tea. I think I'll pour myself a glass; would you like one?"

"If you're having one anyway; sure, I'll take a glass."

She brought the tea out to where Jess was already sitting on the same porch rocker he had vacated earlier.

"You said you're from Maryland. Where did you learn to like sweet iced tea?"

"At the Quilting Bee, of course. Valerie serves it by the gallon." She swatted away a fly that had not quite landed on the rim of her glass, then looked him straight in the eyes. "Chief Hamilton, you didn't come out here to talk about sweet tea, and we didn't get to finish our conversation before you were called back to the office. Now, please tell me, has there been any favorable news about Heather's condition?" It was apparent that she had gathered her thoughts while he was gone.

"She does have a concussion, but the doctor seems to think she'll be fine."

"That's a relief. Has she been able to give you any details yet?"

"Not yet. My deputy is with her as we speak. I'll know something soon." He searched for someplace to set his glass. Not finding a side table beside his rocker, he reached over and placed it on the porch rail, then took a small notebook and pen out of his shirt pocket. He pulled his reading glasses from the lanyard around his neck and put them on, poised to write. "But back to your story. You were getting ready to tell me something important. If I remember correctly, it was about your aunt wanting something bad enough to steal it."

"Yes," she said. "A valuable family heirloom that's been handed down from generation to generation since the 1840's and I was the next in line, skipping my uncle since he had no heirs. While I was in college, my grandmother died, then my grandfather just a year later, the year I graduated. The farm was left to me in a trust and by the time the estate was settled, I had joined the Order. It was supposed to be tied up tight in my grandfather's will that the family heirloom would be passed on to me, but it ended up in the hands of my uncle and his wife. I think they assumed that I had taken the vows of poverty, celibacy and obedience, and wasn't allowed to own anything, which in fact isn't true. I don't know how much you know about the Catholic Church, but nuns and sisters are often mistaken for one and the same, but there is a difference. A Nun lives in a convent within a cloister and takes the vows I just mentioned as *solemn* vows. A Sister, which is what I am, is someone who goes out into the world where we're needed to minister to those outside the convent. We're called *active* or *apostolic* because we take the gospel to others where they are. We profess our *simple* vows and those vows allow us the right to own property, such as an estate or things inherited from a relative. We're not allowed to use them for financial gain, but we can retain ownership of them. Do you understand the difference?"

Jess nodded. "I think so. I had no idea there was a difference between Nuns and Sisters but you've explained it well."

"And most people don't. The terms are pretty much interchangeable. Out in the world, Sisters are almost always called Nuns, and people refer to the Nuns in convents as Sisters. It's only within the Catholic Church that people know the difference." She smiled. "And sometimes not even there." She took a drink of tea, then set the glass back down.

"What did you do with the family farm?"

"I still retain ownership, but it's being leased out to a farmer and his family, and the money from the lease goes to fund charities that our Diocese supports. I'm thinking of diverting a portion of it to help fund our shelter here in Park Place."

"That's generous." Jess was impressed.

She smiled. "I've had no need for it. But back to the family heirloom. I never pushed them for it. If they wanted it bad enough to steal it, let them have it. I had almost forgotten about it until Uncle Al's attorney called me. Uncle Al died several years ago. His attorney happened to see in the obituaries that his wife, Marilee had just passed away, and he started wondering about her will. Then he found out she had chosen to use a different attorney to draw up her will. He remembered the change that Uncle Al made in his will right before he died. He'd had a change of heart. His wife would inherit everything except the most important family heirloom which was to be returned to me upon his death because it was legally mine anyway."

"What happened to it?" Jess asked.

"She ignored the will and kept it. But since it wasn't rightfully hers, she couldn't legally will it to anyone else, but that didn't keep her from trying, which is probably why she switched attorneys." She paused and sighed. "Now it's turned up missing and the lawyer was concerned. That's why I'm here."

Jess was fascinated with her story, but wondered what it had to do with Park Place. His mind was trying to piece together something she had said, but part of the puzzle was missing. "The family heirloom must be valuable. What was it?"

She sat there for a minute, rocking gently back and forth, before she looked at him. "A quilt," she said. "A Baltimore Album Quilt. And it's missing. That's why I came to see you today."

Jess's eyes registered his shock, then he slowly nodded as the puzzle pieces fell in place. "Marilee! When you said it, I knew I'd heard that name before. So, your Uncle Al was Al Bayley and he was married to Marilee Bayley."

"Yes, and my name is Margaret Bayley."

"And your uncle's lawyer was concerned about who?"

"Marilee's nephew and niece. The late Horace Gunter and his cousin Amelia Reinhart."

CHAPTER 27

A PUZZLE SOLVED

Jess was shocked. He'd truly thought that Sister Margaret was going to tell him about some little problem, maybe a theft, or some type of harassment that either she or one of the transients at the homeless shelter was experiencing. He had originally wondered if there was a connection, but that was just grasping at straws. Since he had met her this afternoon, he had ruled her out of having any connection with the quilt at all.

"Go ahead," he said quietly.

"Uncle Al's attorney contacted Marilee's attorney and told him about the original will. He was surprised and said that Marilee had used the quilt to manipulate her niece and nephew, Horace and Amelia. She had changed her will several times, leaving it to Horace one day and Amelia the next. During the reading of the will, Horace and Amelia were both shocked that in the end she had changed her mind completely and willed it to a museum in Baltimore. Maybe she didn't know it didn't legally belong to her." She stopped talking and took a sip of her iced tea. "Or she didn't care."

"That's strange," Jess said. "Her attorney didn't disclose any of that when he spoke to the police in Maryland. He didn't say anything about your uncle's will, only that her final wish was to leave the quilt to the museum. Maybe he was just trying to protect the other attorney since he didn't follow through making sure the quilt got to the rightful owner. It sure would have helped if we'd had that information.

Margaret set her tea glass on the deck rail alongside Jess's and started talking again. "I think eventually both lawyers tried to get the quilt back, but it had disappeared along with both Horace and Amelia."

"But how did you know they were here in Park Place? And what brought you to Park Place?"

"I only knew about Horace. Is Amelia here too? Does she have the quilt? The lawyers thought Horace had it."

She looked hopeful, but Jess didn't answer, so she went on with the story. "Marilee's attorney knew that Horace had her debit card and a checkbook since he was taking care of her bills during her final days. He was her main caregiver, so he must have been a pretty decent person, even though they did suspect him of taking the quilt. The attorneys checked with the bank and the last transaction on the card was to pay for an extended stay motel room not far from here."

"The Queen's Inn."

"Yes, of course you found that out when you were investigating Horace's death." She brushed at the fly that had finally settled on the rim of her glass. Her sudden movement knocked the glass off the rail, but she caught it before it hit the porch.

"Good catch," he said. "And you? What brought you to Park Place?"

"God did." At his skeptical look, she continued. "It really is sort of a miracle that I'm here. The diocese puts out a flyer each month listing available mission opportunities that the Sisters can apply for. That's where

I saw the assignment posted for needing an assistant in the homeless shelter here in town. It was at a time when I had become disheartened with my work." She paused and then looked into his eyes. "To be honest, I had even started questioning my calling. The job sounded appealing so I almost applied to be sent here, but I had also grown complacent so I did nothing about it." She looked down at her hands, then interlocked both hands together flexing her fingers, then put them up to her face as if praying.

Jess was surprised at her confession. Did nuns really question their calling? He'd once had a pastor friend who got out of the ministry because he felt he'd misunderstood his calling.

Margaret put her hands back in her lap with them still interlocked. He was patient and waited for her to speak. After a short while, she did.

"Just a week later, Uncle Al's attorney told me that Horace had been traced to Park Place, the very same town where the position was available. It was as if God was leading me here." She paused again and smiled faintly, "For more than one reason." He wondered what she meant, but didn't have a chance to ask before she continued. "Anyway, I jumped at the chance of trying to find what happened to the quilt, so I applied and got this assignment. Then after I got here, he was murdered and there was no mention of the quilt, I figured he had sold it somewhere between Maryland and here. Providence again, I reasoned. Maybe I had wanted it too much, putting myself first before God. I had done without the quilt all these years, I wasn't going to worry about it now. Besides,

I've grown to love it here and I feel like what I'm doing is worthwhile."

Jess smiled. "You've done a lot already. Did you know that Amelia was here too, at another motel near I-77. I was there this morning."

"No! Do you think she killed Horace?"

"She's our prime suspect."

She shook her head. "That's terrible - her own cousin! I didn't know either of them, only what I heard from my mother and grandparents. I've never called Marilee my aunt, even though she was married to my uncle. There's no blood kin and she made it hard for me to like her. But I never heard anything about Amelia that would lead me to think she was capable of murder."

"Someone else was murdered today. I wish you had come to us when you read about Horace's death in the paper," Jess said. His voice was accusatory and Margaret winced.

"I've been beating myself up over that, which is why I went to the station today. If I'd had any idea that Amelia was here.... but it seems I went to the station too late if someone else was murdered today. Do you know who it was?"

"We have a name, but there's something still puzzling about him. He was a loan shark at the racetrack and Horace owed him money from a line of credit he gave him for placing bets on a horse."

"What is it that you find puzzling?"

He laughed. "Just about everything about this case has been a puzzle until now. Do you know if Amelia had any other relatives besides Horace?"

"It's odd that you asked that," she said. "It's rather complicated, but yes, she has a half brother. Marilee had two sisters, Alice, Amelia's mother, and Ethel, Horace's mother."

"I agree, it's been complicated so far."

She laughed. "I think about my poor mother. She had to deal with the drama whether she wanted to or not. She told me about it just a few years back to explain why she had distanced herself from the family."

"Anyway, when Alice was just sixteen, she was dating a smooth talking Italian boy and got pregnant. She had a baby boy but she was young and wanted nothing to do with him, so his Italian grandparents took him and raised him. A couple of years later, she married and not long after that, Amelia was born. So, Amelia has a half-brother, the one who was raised by his Italian grandparents. I have no idea what his name is or where he is, but I remember my mom saying that when he was born, he had Alice's features and looked nothing like his dad. Why do you ask? Is he somehow involved in this?"

Jess nodded as another piece of puzzle fell into place. "I'm pretty sure he was, especially now that you've said he was Italian. If my hunch is correct, his name is Arlo Balbini and he's in our county morgue, murdered at the hands of his half-sister, Amelia Reinhart."

Her eyes grew bigger and rounder. "You've got to be kidding?"

"I wish I was kidding," he said. "And each of them share a heart-shaped birthmark, just as their cousin Horace did."

Margaret sat in the rocker, looking down at her hands. "And so did their mother, Alice, and Alice's sister, Marilee, and probably Horace's mother although I don't know that for sure. The birthmark was a genetic trait that ran in their family." The realization of what had happened made her hands shake and she looked up at Jess. "I should have come to you in the first place. Maybe none of this would have happened."

"It wouldn't have prevented Horace's death, Margaret, but it would have helped the investigation. But I'm guilty too. I thought it would be best to leave the quilt out of the news and without knowing it was involved in the murder investigation, you didn't feel it necessary to come forward."

"You mean, Horace didn't sell the quilt? Where is it?"

"It's a long story."

"Longer than mine?"

Jess looked over the top of his reading glasses and arched his eyebrows. "I don't think that's possible," he said. "You've filled up my notebook."

She laughed, an infectious little laugh; the first he'd heard from her since they began their somber conversation.

He put his notebook and pen back in his pocket. Standing up, he took off his reading glasses, once again letting them dangle from his neckstrap. He picked up his glass of tea and drank several gulps in succession. "Don't worry about the quilt, Sister Margaret. Right now, it's being held as State's evidence, but it'll be returned to you once the trial is over." He drained the glass and set it back on the rail.

"I'm happy that it wasn't sold or pawned", she said, "but I'm afraid that quilt would bring me nothing but sad memories since it's been the object behind all this violence. I'm thinking of respecting Marilee's wishes from her last will and donating it to the Baltimore Art Museum. They would give it the recognition it deserves and keep it preserved. They have a huge collection of Baltimore Album quilts."

"Give yourself some time; you may change your mind. It's always been my way of thinking that heirlooms should be used and enjoyed. Isn't that what your grandparents thought when they specified that you would be the heir? Good memories can triumph over bad memories."

"Thanks for reminding me of them, Chief Hamilton. I do have wonderful memories of time spent with them." They were standing beside his patrol car. "Oh, and another thing...." She blushed and looked down at her hands. "Thank you for allowing Clarence some free time to come out and help me paint. I couldn't have finished so quickly without him."

"Uh...., you're welcome." Clarence had helped paint? When? Not that it was any of his business what Clarence did in his spare time. He was volunteering his time at the police department. He got in his car and started backing up as she walked back to the rectory. When he got back on the street, he started talking aloud. "You sly old dog, Clarence. What kind of trouble are you getting yourself in to?" He mulled it over in his mind as he drove. "Well you can just get yourself out of it. Don't you think for a minute I'm going to get involved." He took a right turn, bypassing the station and driving in the direction of the hospital. "I'm going to see Heather myself. She'll think I've abandoned her."

CHAPTER 28

QUICK-DRAW MCGRAW

The door to Heather's room was open but Jess knocked anyway. "Anybody home?" he asked.

"Come on in!" He was glad to hear Heather's voice and he walked inside. She was sitting on the side of the bed, dressed in the same clothes she had worn to work that morning. "I would jump up and hug you if I could," she said, giving him a dazzling smile. "Doctor's orders though - no sudden moves until this dizziness goes away completely."

"Then I'll hug you," he said, reaching down, giving her a brief hug as if she would break if he hugged any harder. "Looks like you're ready to go home," he said.

"Yes, and I can't wait to get out of here. Dad has gone to pull the car around front, and Mom is at the nurse's station signing me out. They should be bringing a wheelchair in here any minute."

"So, I made it just in time then?"

"Yeah, Cliff left just a few minutes ago. He said you'd gone out to see Sister Margaret. Did she tell you about our visit?"

"Yes, she did. Now I want to hear all about your ordeal. You must have been frightened out of your mind?"

"Are you kidding me! That's the most excitement I've had since I started working at the station!"

He shook his head and rolled his eyes. "Why am I not surprised?"

"Maybe you should promote me to deputy?"

"I think I'll promote you to chief, then I can take over Luther's Barber Shop. I heard he's retiring."

She laughed. "Then the town would be in trouble," she said. "I'd round 'em all up with my six-shooter and you'd give 'em a buzz cut. We'd make a good team."

He laughed as she mimicked a western-style sheriff doing a fast draw. "We already do make a good team", he said. "A regular Quick-Draw McGraw. You get well so you can come back to work and keep us boys from getting into trouble."

"Yes sir!" Her smile turned to concern. "To be honest, I was frightened, Jess. Having a loaded gun pointed at you is a scary experience. Cliff told me about the second murder - the loan shark, wasn't it?" He nodded. "So, you think Amelia Reinhart did it?"

"I'm sure of it," he said. "But you know the process - innocent until proven guilty." They both turned at the sound of a bump at the door.

"Sorry about that," Heather's mom said, as she pushed a wheelchair into the room. "I'm not a very good driver." She bumped the wheelchair again, this time at the foot of the bed."

"Well, I sure hope you're not going to be the one pushing me downstairs. I'm liable to get another concussion."

A nurse had walked in behind her. "Don't worry, Heather. I'll do the driving."

"I'll just slip on out," Jess said. "Heather, I'll catch you up on everything later. We'll be glad to have you back at work."

"Don't mess anything up while I'm out," she called as he walked out the door.

It was after six, but Clarence was still there, sitting at Heather's desk, when Jess walked into the station. His entire expression was a question waiting to be answered, with lines of worry furrowing his brows.

"Well?" he asked.

Jess didn't know where to start. "I just got back from the hospital," he said. "Heather's on her way home."

Clarence's brow furrowed even further as he looked Jess straight in the eyes. "I'm happy about that," he said, "but you know that's not what I was waiting to hear."

It was then that Jess knew for certain, and he nodded his head. "There's someone over at St. Gabriel's that I'm sure would love to talk to you. I think she can tell the story a whole lot better than I can."

Heather's office chair turned over as Clarence pushed back from the desk and pushed it aside. He hurriedly picked it up and set it back up in its right place. "Sorry," he said, and smiled sheepishly. "I have somewhere important I need to be." With that, he hurried out the door, leaving his crumpled raincoat behind.

"Wait", Jess shouted. He hurriedly picked up the raincoat off the chair, but it was too late, Clarence was halfway across the parking lot. He watched the retreating figure and sighed, then watched as the dark clouds that had been gathering broke loose.

Cliff walked into the room. "I heard you calling out," he said. "Were you talking to me?"

"No, I was trying to catch Clarence before he left. I don't know what's got into our Columbo lately. The one day it's rained since he's been on the force, and he runs out without the raincoat."

***

Rain was pounding on the roof of the church office. "Thank You, thank You", Father Thomas said, looking skyward. As he walked over to close the windows, he saw a car drive up to the front of the old rectory. He smiled when he saw who it was. When Margaret had first approached him for counseling, he had been bent on trying to change her mind, but after their many talks and later meeting with the two of them together, he felt at peace. Many of his fellow priests would have counseled them differently, he knew, but he'd witnessed something special between those two and found it hard to believe that it was not of God's choosing. The car door opened and he saw Clarence make a mad dash for the door of the shelter. Why on earth didn't he have on a raincoat, or at least an umbrella. Oh well, love is foolish they say. He closed the last window and walked back to his desk, humming an old Frank Sinatra tune, something about a foolish heart, but he couldn't quite remember the words.

CHAPTER 29

I'LL BRING THE CORNBREAD

After nearly a month of warm weather, a cold front was hovering over Park Place and had no plans to leave anytime soon. It was the coldest April anyone could remember and had folks scrambling to cover up their tender plants with rolls of black plastic to keep them from getting frostbit. Crowder Feed and Seed was selling the plastic as fast as they could get it ordered.

"I keep tellin' them every year not to plant tomatoes outside until May 1st, but can they wait? No siree, they cain't. They just gotta get 'em in the ground." Junie Crowder was complaining to the men who gathered in his store every Monday morning, as Kathleen put it, to chew the fat.

"Quit your harping, Junie," Cap Price said as he sat down on a feed bag that he had pulled out from a shelf. "You've already sold the first round of tomato plants all over town. If they get frostbit, you can double your money by selling 'em more."

"I know it. I just hate to see those little plants I started from seeds and pampered along until they were planting size, shrivel up and die. It's a downright shame."

"But they're covering them up," Larry Braswell piped in. "They shouldn't die."

"It's fine to cover 'em up, but half the dad-blamed town forgets to uncover 'em during the day when the sun gets hot, then they die anyway."

"Just be happy our sales are picking up," Kathleen said, coming out from the back with a plate of brownies. "Here, have one of these. It'll sweeten you up."

"Fatten him up is more like it," Cap said, grabbing one as she passed the plate. "Don't tell Madge I ate a brownie. She's got me on a diet."

Kathleen put the brownies on the counter and covered them up with aluminum foil. "Y'all save one of these for Rev Rock. He'll be in here after a while."

***

"It's really happening this time," Betty said as she opened the cash drawer and pulled out a book of stamps.

"That's what you've been saying for two years," Rock said as he handed her a ten-dollar bill. "I'll believe it when I see it."

"Well, you just sashay yourself in here on Monday morning and you'll see a new face behind this counter, that's what you'll see. Then you'll wish you'd told me a proper goodbye."

"I think she means it." Betty Ann Williams was waiting her turn at the counter and Wanda Burns was standing in the background with her camera. "Get over there closer to Betty, Rev Rock, so I can take your picture. Betty Ann, you get on the other side. I'll print you all a copy as a momento. It may be the last opportunity to get your picture made together."

"Oh shush," Betty said. "I don't want my picture made with him. He doesn't even believe me when I tell

234 | *The Sweet Tea Quilting Bee*

him I'm leaving." As a tear started rolling down her cheek, Rock began to panic.

"No way," he said, this time not so sure. "They wouldn't just pull the rug out from under you with no notice!" She didn't say anything. "Would they?"

"They would and they did," she said, this time not bothering to hide the few tears. "They let me come out of retirement last time because they were cutting back on the post office hours here in Park Place. But now they want to increase my hours without increasing my pay. Forget that! I'll be a lot better off financially if I retire than if I keep working."

At his look of dismay, she sniffled and smiled through her tears. "But y'all can't get rid of me that easy. I'll still come up here and visit, and I'm not beyond eating lunch with the lot of you now and then." She seemed to be getting her bravado back and started talking a little louder. "And I expect real food, too, not some little quiche or spaghetti kind of stuff. And I don't like those french sounding dishes with a dollop of food here and there drizzled with some fancy little sauces. I like fried chicken and pork chops, collard greens and cornbread, oh, and meatloaf and smashed potatoes. Shoot, I'm getting hungry just thinking about it."

"I'll bring the cornbread," Wanda said.

"And I'll bring the collards," Betty Ann said.

"I guess that leaves me bringing the fried chicken," Rock said.

"And don't you go bringing no KFC," Betty said. "I know real fried chicken when I see it."

They all laughed and the mood lightened considerably, except for Rock's. He waited until Betty Ann took their picture with a silly grin plastered on his face, then made his way slowly out the door. As the others were still talking, he was wondering what in the world they would do without Betty. As if he didn't have enough on his mind already. Not one, but two murders had occurred within the confines of Park Place Township. All this in the little town whose reputation had been squeaky clean with not much more than traffic stops and a petty theft or two over the last few years, unless you counted the time Mary Jo Hilton had tried to poison him and had inadvertently poisoned his cat instead. Poor Theo. The town had always been known as the little town with a big heart and he hoped this wouldn't tarnish that image.

He picked up his pace as he continued walking down the street. It was Monday morning and he had a busy schedule ahead of him. Three appointments this afternoon and two of them were couples wanting to join the church - a good thing indeed! And then there was that appointment tomorrow morning with Sister Margaret from St. Gabriel's. He'd already asked and received approval from session to give another donation to the shelter so that should put a smile on her face. It was certainly a worthwhile program. Why, he'd heard this morning that Mitzi Barlow and her three children had gone to the shelter just last night when their landlord had evicted the young mother for not paying rent. It was likely to be a long-term stay for them and thank goodness, the shelter was prepared for things like that. The Barlows weren't members of Park Place Presbyterian, but that didn't stop him from wanting to get his hands ahold of her no-good husband for walking out on his family, taking the rent money with him and buying a ring for his new girlfriend. Lord, help them all, he said in a silent prayer.

He stopped in front of Crowder's Feed and Seed and peered in. Yes, the men were all there. He looked at his watch. He had a few minutes to spare. He might as well go in and see what the gossip was about today. Maybe he could contribute to it with the news about Betty. If he didn't start crying again, that is.

***

Jess walked out of The Banty Hen with a plate of chocolate chip cookies in his hand and got in his squad car. He watched as Rev Rock stopped and peered in the Feed and Seed and then watched him walk in. He smiled, thinking about the men who had passed the time on Monday mornings with Junie and Kathleen. They had an old wood stove they would crank up in the winter and would pull up rickety chairs and horse feed bags so they could waste away half a day in the companionship of old friends. He should go in and sit a spell, but Cliff and Clarence were waiting on him to get back to the station. Heather was finally feeling well enough to come back and they all wanted to do a little something to welcome her back. Valerie had made some cookies for the occasion and Cliff had picked up some flowers and balloons at May's Flower Shop. Clarence was making a pot of coffee, and it sure would feel good to have some on this cold, blustery day in late April. Channel 3's weatherman had said this morning that it was the latest frost on record.

***

The cookies had been eaten and two balloons had escaped the confinement of the string that held them together and were now hugging the ceiling with their strings hanging just out of reach. Heather, Jess, Clarence and Cliff were gathered around a small folding table in Clarence's office enjoying their coffee and talking about the murders, now solved.

"I'm just glad it's all over," Cliff said. "Maybe we can get back to normal now."

"You know," Heather said. "I didn't realize how much of a blow this was to the businesses on Main Street. I've had lots of visitors at Mama's house since my whack on the head and this murder business really affected the whole town. May, at the flower shop, said her business was off because people were afraid to walk downtown alone. Moms were afraid for their children to play outside by themselves and that's never been the case here in Park Place. It's about as safe as you can get. It makes you realize that violent crimes can happen anywhere. Who would have ever thought it would happen here?"

"I never heard the full story of what happened to you, Heather," Clarence said. "Start from the beginning."

Heather grinned. She loved telling the story. "Well, I was sitting here minding my own business. Sister Margaret had been here and left. She said she heard something, but I dismissed it, thinking it was just house-settling noises like we hear all the time, but someone must have come in while we were talking. I think they were hiding in the closet as you come in the front door. After Sister Margaret left, I dialed my home phone number and talked to the dogs."

Jess had heard it before and was amused at the way Clarence reacted.

"Did I hear you right?" he asked. "How did you talk to your dogs?"

"I talked to them on my answering machine, Silly. It calms them down to hear me talking to them in the middle of the day."

Clarence popped himself on the side of his head. "Oh yes, how could I be so stupid. I'm sure everyone talks to their dogs on their answering machines."

"Well, if they don't, they should. Anyway, that's when he walked in. I told Buster and Brandy I had to go, and hung up the phone."

Jess laughed out loud and Heather gave him a mean look. "If y'all don't stop interrupting, it'll take all day."

"Sorry, I won't interrupt again," he said, still snickering.

"Please don't," she said, but her tone was teasing. "Anyway, the man asked for you, Jess, and I told him you would be back soon. Then he asked where was the quilt. That's when I knew something was wrong because nobody was supposed to know about the quilt. I tried to back up so that I could escape to your office and lock myself in there, but he caught me by the wrist and knocked my Mama's pretty tulips over. I told him I didn't know where the quilt was, but he said he knew it was in the basement and asked where was the key. I pointed to your office. He made me go in with him. After he ransacked it and didn't find the key, he threatened me with his gun, so I got my key out. He was right behind me as I made my way down the steps and when I got to the bottom, I just remember being hit from behind with the gun, or I assumed it was the gun since it was the only thing he had in his hand. The next thing I remember, I was in the hospital."

"Were you afraid?" Cliff asked.

"Well, duh! Wouldn't you be?"

Jess watched as the two of them bantered back and forth, and thought how blessed they were that Heather hadn't been hurt any worse. Yes, he was glad it was all over, too, but it wouldn't really be over until the trial. In the meanwhile, Amelia Reinhart was sitting in the county jail stewing over what was to happen to her. All because of a quilt!

CHAPTER 30

ANOTHER REALM

"I feel like the weight of the world has been lifted from my shoulders," Valerie said as she and Sam finished setting up the chairs in the quilting room. "I didn't realize how much fear I'd been living under all this while until Jess told us they had the crazy quilt lady in custody."

"Me too, Valerie. It was stressful having to look over our shoulders all the time, worrying about what lurked behind the shadows whenever we heard the door open or close. And to think, we probably had two different murderers in our shop several times over the last few weeks. We're lucky we weren't victims ourselves."

"You don't know how much I've thought about that, Sam. For a while there we thought they could be one and the same person because of the identical birthmarks, but knowing they're half-siblings somehow makes it worse. What makes a person kill her own brother?"

"Greed, one of the oldest sins in the world. Always wanting something you can't have, like Eve wanting the forbidden apple in the Garden of Eden."

"Hey, you forget that Adam wasn't a saint through all that. Eve didn't force him to take a bite of that old apple."

Sam laughed. "No, but she must have been mighty convincing, just like you can be sometimes."

She smiled coyly at him. "Like when I give you my best 'come hither' look?" She batted her eyes.

"Yes, that's it," he said. "You win me over every time." He pushed the last chair up against a small white table. "There, we've finished."

"What I still don't understand is who killed poor Horace? Was it the crazy quilt lady or the antique fishing lure man?" she asked.

He chuckled at her descriptions. "I think you're safe to call them Amelia Reinhart and Arlo Balbini now, but back to your question. They may never know which one of them killed Horace. Jess says that Amelia blames it on Balbini, but I would too if I were in her position. She's likely to get a much longer sentence if she's found guilty of committing two murders. With one, she may have a chance to be eligible for parole someday."

"I sure don't want to see her face in here again," Valerie said.

"I think I'll put on a pot of coffee," Sam said. "As cold as it is out there, some of the ladies may want something warm to drink."

"That sounds good. The iced tea is in the fridge and it's decaffeinated. Holly isn't drinking caffeine now that she's expecting a baby. The chime on the door rang and they both walked out of the room together to see who it was.

"Oh look, it's Sister Margaret, and she's out of her habit again today. She looks nice in street clothes."

"Yes she does," Sam said. "It makes you notice how pretty she is."

"She is quite pretty, isn't she?"

Margaret saw them and waved. Valerie walked to the front to meet her. "Sister Margaret, how good to see you!

You can go on back to the quilting room or you can browse around while we get the refreshments on the table."

"It's good to see you too, Valerie. I brought us a special treat today to celebrate." She opened the box she was carrying and a delicious aroma filled the air. "One of my mother's favorite recipes - orange dreamsicle scones."

Valerie looked surprised. "Oh, does the Mother Superior bake?"

Margaret smiled with a hint of mischief. "Not normally," she said. "You do know that nuns have real mothers, don't you?"

Valerie blushed. "Oh, of course you do! Forgive me, I'm sort of ditzy sometimes. I guess I think of you Sisters as belonging to another realm, like angels or something."

"Oh no, I'm afraid nuns are very human. We try to lead the lives God calls us to, but it's not always easy, and...." She paused as if she'd said too much. "You know Valerie, you remind me a lot of my own mother."

Valerie took the scones from her and they started walking to the quilting room. "I'll take that as a compliment! Oh, I forgot to ask. What are we celebrating?"

"Finishing our baby quilts. Lydia said we'd be sewing the binding on today. I think we've come a long way since that awkward moment when a nun dressed in full habit made a grand appearance in the middle of your first quilting class."

"And what a lucky day that was for us!" She put the scones on the table. "These will be so much better if I keep them warm. I think I have a hot pad in the back. I'll warm it up in the microwave and put it on top of the box. I'll be right back."

When she came back, she had the hot pad and a plate of cookies. Sam was right behind her with the coffee pot ready to plug in. "I'll be right back with the tea," he said.

Valerie put the heated hot pad on top of the box of scones and Margaret started filling the glasses with ice. By the time they finished, the others started trickling in the front door. Sam brought the tea pitcher in and then went out to greet them. Margaret turned and smiled at Valerie. "Thank you for making me feel welcome in your group. A nun's life can be lonely."

"I'm so glad you walked through the door that day! I never dreamed I would be good friends with a nun." She put her hand up to her mouth. "There I go again! But you know what I mean."

Margaret laughed. "Don't apologize, I do know what you mean. We do seem to have the reputation of being untouchable, but I think it's a lot to do with how we dress. It seems so formal, somehow, like a long flowing tuxedo. I've noticed that all of you seem to respond to me differently when I'm in casual clothes and I like that."

"You know, I haven't thought of it that way; it's true!" She pointed to the others as they made their way to the back. "Look at us. We're from all walks of life and we span several decades. We're so very different, yet we have so much in common when we get right down to it. We all have interesting stories to tell, don't we?"

"Yes, very interesting, I'm sure."

The murders were the main topic of the conversation after they had helped themselves and oohed and aahed over Margaret's scones. No one, not even Valerie knew about Sister Margaret's connection with the quilt. The ladies were naturally curious and with the arrest made and everything out in the open, Valerie was free to discuss the role the antique shop played in the story.

Madge shook her head. "Wow, you and Sam could have been hurt. What is the world coming to?"

"I think all of us can rest easier now that they've solved the murders," Holly said. "I haven't let Abby play outside by herself since the poor old man was killed. And to think a woman was responsible! Do they think she killed both victims?"

"Oh, I wish Rebecca was here. I'm sure she knows more than I do. From what I've heard, the woman blames the other man for killing Mr. Gunther, although the coroner's report says he died from a heart attack. Then the woman, her name was Amelia, killed the man who it turns out was her half-brother. It's all so complicated and I don't think Jess has told me the whole story. But they both have been right here inside this building!" She turned to her new friend from Sun's Up. "Kay, you met Amelia here in the shop. She was here the same day you suggested starting a quilter's club. Do you remember?"

"The woman who was so rude?"

"That's the one. And she was persistent, coming back again and being equally as rude the next time. She was looking for antique quilts and little did I know she was looking for the same quilt that Mr. Gunther was trying to sell us when he came in the shop before his murder. And the the other man had been here too, sneaking around looking through boxes and such."

"How can a person be so greedy that they would kill someone over a quilt of all things? Was the quilt valuable?"

"Very valuable." She told them the story as she knew it from start to finish, not leaving out a single detail and even embellishing a few things for special effect. "I get cold chills when I think of those dangerous criminals coming back and forth into our shop. Why, we could have been murdered ourselves!"

Sam was dusting the shelves where the pink and green depression glass was displayed right outside the door to the quilting room. He had been smiling as his wife relished in telling the ladies all about it, but her last sentence was sobering. They really had been in danger! What if they had paid poor Horace the thousand dollars he wanted for the quilt when he first came into the shop? And what if they had displayed it in the shop the same day? Instead of killing poor Horace, the duo may have come in and robbed the store. It would be easy to do and the murderer seemed to have no scruples at all. He shuddered to think what would have happened and then bowed his head thanking the good Lord that He had kept them safe. He said an extra prayer hoping to intercede for Valerie just in case those little embellishments she told were sinful.

Margaret had sat quietly throughout the discussions. Jess had thought it best to keep her involvement in the story out of the news. He hadn't told anyone outside the police department and she was grateful. It was hard enough knowing that the quilt that should have brought joy to the eyes of the beholder had wreaked so much havoc at the hands of those who were greedy.

***

The bindings had been sewn around the edges of the quilt and the sewing machines were finally silent. "We really are finished!" The quilt Jenny Braswell was holding up was alive with color.

"Let's have Sam come in and take our pictures," Valerie said.

Maura reached down in her purse. "I've got my camera. I was planning to take some pictures anyway."

"I'll find Sam." Valerie stuck her head out the door and started to call his name. "Oh, there you are," she said, seeing him dusting the shelves near the door. "Have you been spying on us?"

"Now, whyever would I want to do that?" He smiled and laid the duster down on the shelf and walked into the room behind Valerie. "Just give me a camera." Maura handed it over. The sewing partners each held their quilts between them.

"Wow," Sam said, admiring the play of light in the room. "The lighting in here is perfect to display quilts. We'll have to keep that in mind, Valerie. Maybe we *should* buy more quilts."

"Don't you start too, Sam!"

The sun shining through the century-old mullioned windows cast a brilliant diamond-shaped pattern on the original heart-pine floors. The mirrors in the room reflected the light and bounced it from quilt to quilt creating a warm, rich glow in the room. Sam took pictures, first individually and then lined them all up as a group. When he got to Madge, he had to pause long enough for her to put on her bright red lipstick.

"I'll send some digital prints to the Gazette. Maybe you ladies will end up on the front page."

Holly walked around the room looking at each quilt. "They're beautiful. Actually, they're amazing considering some of our group are first time quilters. Of course, it helped that we paired the oldies with the newbies. I'm volunteering at the hospital tomorrow and I'll let the Administrator know we're finished. When we got initial approval to donate the quilts to the nursery, she mentioned it would be good publicity if we had a dedication ceremony."

"That would be nice", Valerie said.

"Okay ladies, what do you want to start next?" Lydia asked. "Do you want to tackle something more difficult than baby quilts?"

There was a lot of talking at once and Sam tiptoed out of the room unnoticed.

CHAPTER 31

RIGHT ON TIME

Rock looked at his watch. It was exactly 9:58 a.m., just two minutes shy of Sister Margaret's appointment time. He got up from his desk and stretched, then walked into the outer office, walking past Reva's vacant chair and over to the window facing the parking lot. It had rained last night and the paved lot was full of puddles.

Reva had taken her husband, Walter for a doctor's appointment and Rock had been answering phone calls all morning. Holly had volunteered to come over to answer the phone while Reva was gone, but he'd told her he could handle them until his appointment at ten. And there she was, walking across the parking lot exactly on time. It was a short walk since she, Sonny and little Abby lived in the cottage behind the church that had once been the manse. He had recently found out they were expecting a new baby and he was thrilled for them.

He watched as she stopped and waited for a car that was pulling into the parking lot. It was Clarence Foster's car. Uh, oh, had he overbooked appointments? He looked on Reva's calendar. No, just the appointment for Sister Margaret was pencilled in on hers too. Oh well, Clarence would just have to wait. He watched as Clarence got out of the driver's side door and walked around the car to the passenger side. In just a moment, he walked back around the car with a younger woman beside him.

Could it be his daughter, he wondered? No, he'd met his daughter when Teresa passed away. She was in her late twenties and this woman was closer to Liz's age. Ahh, maybe he had a new romantic interest.

He watched as Holly walked up to them and then noticed that Holly hugged the young woman. It was apparently someone she knew from the way they chatted amicably. He had made a fresh pot of coffee in case Sister Margaret wanted some, so he walked over to the cabinet and pulled out several cups. He would find out what they wanted and if they wanted to sit out his appointment with the nun, that was fine. He looked at the clock above the door. 10:05. If she was running late, he could talk to Clarence for just a few minutes. If it required more time, Clarence would have to wait or come back.

The door opened, and the three of them walked in, with the two women still chatting. When they saw Rock, they stopped talking.

"Come on inside where it's warm," Rock said. "It's still pretty chilly outside." Clarence walked in last and closed the door.

"Holly, thanks for coming. The phones have been busy all morning." He turned to Clarence. "And Clarence, my friend, to what do I owe the pleasure of your company today? And your friend?" He turned to the young woman. "I don't think we've met before." He stuck out his hand for a handshake. She took it, looking at the clock.

"I'm sorry, I'm a few minutes late for my appointment," she said.

Rock's eyes widened. "Hmm," he said. "I don't think we have an appointment, unless my secretary, Reva set it by mistake. I have another appointment that should be arriving in a few minutes." He recovered from his confusion. "But until she does, I'll be happy to talk to you." He turned to Clarence. "What about you Clarence?" Clarence shrugged and smiled, the corners of his mouth upturning in mischief.

"Oh, I'm so sorry," the woman said. "I'm your 10 o'clock appointment, but how could you know who I am? I don't have on my habit. I'm Margaret. I talked to you last week"

Rock felt like he could have been knocked over with a feather. "You're Sister Margaret?" he asked, with an incredulous look on his face.

The corners of her mouth upturned, just as Clarence's had done. "Well, not exactly," she said, looking over at Clarence. He nodded to her in encouragement. "I was Sister Margaret when I made the appointment." Her voice cracked with emotion.

Rock saw that Holly was looking at her with as much confusion as he felt. "I'm afraid I don't understand," he said.

"Now I'm just plain Margaret, but I'd rather be called Maggie."

"I'm sorry, Maggie. Where are my manners. Since we have an appointment, let's go back to my office." He glanced at Clarence. "Did you want Clarence to come back with you?" He still didn't know what Clarence had to do with this, but he thought he'd offer.

"No, I'm fine. I just brought him along for moral support."

She no sooner got seated in the chair in front of Rock's desk when she began to talk again. "I hope you'll forgive me. I didn't mean to confuse you. When I made the appointment with you, I didn't know things would be happening so quickly. I've asked to be released from my vows and I am leaving the Order."

Rock was surprised, but had finally gathered his thoughts. He didn't comment, and waited for her to go on. He saw a tear rolling down her cheek and got up from his chair to hand her a box of tissues. "I wasn't expecting to be so emotional," she said. She used the tissue to wipe the tear away, then put her hands in her lap, a natural gesture. Her posture was perfect and she seemed to have composed herself.

"I've been struggling with this for several months," she said. "I've been happy with my life as a nun but now, in the same way that I'd felt a calling to be a nun, I've been gradually feeling a pull toward an ordinary life. Recently, I've felt like God's calling me to serve Him in some other way, and I've felt such a strong sense of longing for something else. I didn't fully realize what it was until I met Clarence. God spoke to me, He really did, Reverend Clark, and He told me to follow my heart. I didn't happen upon this decision lightly. I've spent many hours in prayer. There's no doubt in my mind that His calling is real and through Him I've made the right decision."

"I gather you've talked to Father Thomas since you seem to have all the steps in place to leave the Order?"

She gave a quick laugh. "Yes, and he wasn't nearly as surprised as I thought he'd be. He said that ever since I

252 | *The Sweet Tea Quilting Bee*

came here, he had sensed a certain restlessness and I didn't fit the mold of a typical Sister, whatever that's supposed to mean." She rolled her eyes and Rock laughed. "I wanted to tell him that Sisters are individuals and no two are alike. We're not robots and we're not all cut from the same mold, but I didn't have the nerve. Besides, I didn't want to get on his bad side." She saw the humor in Rock's eyes and wondered if she'd said too much. "Not that he has a bad side. He's been very good to me and I value the advice he gave and the many prayers he petitioned for my sake. And most importantly, he believed me and accepted the fact that I was being called by God in a new direction."

Rock could see and feel her sincerity. Her eyes were pleading for him to understand, and he did because he had felt God's calling many times in his own life. When it's right, you know it's right.

"Where does Clarence fit into all this?" he asked. He had to know. If she was asking for advice, he needed to know the facts.

She smiled. "I was struggling with this long before I met Clarence, but when he walked in the door of the shelter one afternoon and rescued me from the rickety old ladder I was standing on, I felt an immediate connection of spirit. As I've prayed about this, I've found that I still have my deep yearning for the intimate relationship I have with God, but He's shown me that I have room in my heart now for a deeper relationship with another human; something much more than the active ministry of being a Sister in a religious order."

"And how does Clarence feel?" he asked.

She smiled. "Why don't we ask him?"

Rock knew love when he saw it. After all, he was still reveling in it after being married to Liz for two years. When Clarence came in, he pulled a chair as close as possible to where Margaret sat. As soon as he sat down, he took her hand in his. The tender look he gave her was all that was necessary to give his feelings away. Rock smiled inwardly. Yep, he was in love alright.

"Rock, you don't know how hard I fought this attraction. I even felt guilty that I was somehow betraying the love Teresa and I had shared, and as I've told you before, Teresa was the love of my life."

Rock glanced over to see how Margaret would react to this profession of love for his deceased wife. She sensed his questioning look. "Don't worry," she told him. "My commitment to my calling over the years has taught me to never be envious. There's no legitimate place in the human heart for envy. It destroys from the inside out. Hearing about Clarence's love and commitment to his wife just validates what I already know about him. He's a good and faithful man, both to God and to those he loves."

"Your experience has certainly given you wisdom and clarity," Rock said. Then looking back at Clarence, he smiled and said, "You've got a lot to live up to, my friend. She has a pretty high opinion of you."

"Love is blind," he said, laughing, "but I'll do my best." He told Rock about going to St. Gabriel's under the guise of finding out more about the homeless shelter, but that he was really checking out some of the tall, thin people known to be in town.

"We had interviewed everyone on Main Street and the term *tall and thin* came up in just about every description of the stranger seen around town the day before the death of Horace Gunther. Cliff had told me and Jess that the new nun in town was tall and thin. Since nothing else had panned out, we didn't want to rule anyone out even though interviewing a nun was stretching it a little bit. When I walked into the rectory that day, someone was perched precariously on the top rung of a ladder, painting the walls. My first thought was that she was going to fall and I rushed over. I held the ladder as she came down and when she took her last step and turned to face me, my knees turned to jelly. It was as if God was giving me a glimpse of good things to come. She was wearing overalls and I had no idea who she was. When I found out she was Sister Margaret, I knew it wouldn't work. She had already accepted a higher calling. I could never steal her away from a calling that God Himself had orchestrated. I fought my feelings, but they just wouldn't go away. I was beginning to think the old devil himself was behind it all but then again, the feeling wasn't lustful, it just seemed..., well it just seemed right. It's hard to describe. And of course, I ruled Maggie out as a suspect right then and there. I started going by the shelter on my days off to help paint and as we worked together and got to know each other, she revealed that God had been leading her in a different direction, and I hoped against all odds that the direction was to cross paths with me." He held his hands up in the air. "And this is where we are now." He looked at her and took her hand once more. "We're happy and in love and just as soon as her paperwork comes back saying she's released from her vows, we plan to get married."

"I'm sure God has something wonderful in store for the two of you," Rock said. It was all he knew to say. He was happy for them, but it saddened him that here was another one of God's servants giving up her calling of ministering to others, just as pastors of all faiths seemed to be dropping out at an alarming rate.

"I understand what you're thinking, Reverend Clark." She paused. "Or would you prefer that I call you Rev Rock?"

He wondered how she could possibly know what he was thinking when he really wasn't sure himself. "Please do, that's what everyone calls me."

"I'm leaving the Order, but I'm not leaving the ministry. I've already committed to Father Thomas that I'll continue my work with the homeless shelter however long he needs me on a volunteer basis. I've loved every minute of my work here."

"You've read my mind, Maggie." He turned to Clarence. "And that means you, my friend, can get yourself in a heap of trouble if she starts reading yours."

Clarence laughed. "I'll admit, that's pretty scary. I won't have much time to get in trouble though. She's already recruited me to help at the shelter. Once the trial is out of the way, Jess and Cliff can go back to the way things were and we'll keep our fingers crossed that the crime spree is over in Park Place. I'll be there for another week or two to help them wrap things up. Jess has his hands full right now."

"Greed does strange things to people. We need a little peace and quiet around here now."

Clarence stood up. "Thank you for taking the time to talk to us, Rev Rock. We wanted to explain things before you heard it from someone else."

Maggie stayed seated. "Aren't you forgetting something?" she asked. Clarence looked at her in confusion. "You forgot to ask him...."

"Oh, yeah. I don't want to forget the most important thing. Rock, we'd like for you to marry us."

"I'm flattered," he said. "When do you want the wedding to take place?"

"I'd like to get married tomorrow," he said looking at Margaret, "but we'll need to wait until her release is finalized. They said it could be two weeks or two months."

"Good, I was going to suggest several counseling sessions before the marriage. This is going to be a big step for both of you and before I can be comfortable in performing the ceremony, I want to be sure you're ready for it."

"I trust your judgement," Clarence said. "I wouldn't want it any other way."

Rock turned to Maggie. "Do you plan to continue worshiping in the Catholic faith after your marriage, or have you made that decision? And what about you, Clarence? I think it's important that you worship together, no matter what denomination you choose."

"We've discussed it and we've decided to worship here at Park Place Presbyterian. It's already going to be a big transition for me, so I'm not going to drop out of the Catholic Church completely just yet. I'll still go to Mass, but on Sundays, I'll worship here with Clarence."

"That sounds fair enough." They stood up to leave. Rock stood too and reached for Maggie's hand. "You know I wish nothing but the best for the two of you. Congratulations! Do you mind if I pray with you?"

"Please do," Clarence said.

Rock prayed a heartfelt prayer and ended with 1 Corinthians 13:13, "*And now these three remain: faith, hope and love. But the greatest of these is love.*" He lifted his head and touched each one of them on the shoulder. "And now, my friends, go in peace and may the peace of God go with you."

They walked out the door holding hands, each dabbing at their eyes with a tissue.

CHAPTER 32

MALICIOUS INTENT

"Mrs. Balbini is squealing like a pig. She's never liked Amelia and says she's the whole reason Arlo got involved in the first place."

"How did he get involved, Jess? I've been wondering if it was just a coincidence that the fellow Horace borrowed money from just happened to be the half-brother of Amelia." After taking a few days off, Clarence had come by the station to catch up.

"No, it wasn't a coincidence. When old Mrs. Bayley died, Horace was apparently so sure that he was going to inherit the quilt, he decided to put more money on the horse races than he normally did, thinking he could easily sell it before he had to pay the loan back. He and Amelia were on halfway friendly terms. It was before the will was read. She told him to get in touch with her half-brother; he was in the money loaning business. And so he did. Borrowed $800 from him, but he forgot to read the fine print. Loan sharks typically charge 20% interest with only a month to pay it back. Long story, short, neither Horace nor Amelia inherited the quilt and Amelia had sneaked in her aunt's house and stolen it. Horace then ransacked Amelia's house and took it for himself. Then she had Balbini search Horace's house to get it back, but by that time Horace had left the state. And that's when they both went after him. Here, in Park Place of all towns!"

"Wow," Clarence said, somber at the thought. "There was a whole lot of quilt stealing going on. Did Mrs. Balbini have an answer to which of them killed Horace?"

"She claims it was Amelia and I'm inclined to agree with her." He got up out of his chair and started pacing the floor. "You know what's frustrating? We could charge Amelia with murder in Horace's death, but since there are no witnesses it would be hard to prove. Now I'm afraid they're going to let her plea bargain and get off with a lighter sentence than she should. This was her own half-brother, for heaven's sake! The SLED agent says she could get away with serving as little as ten years behind bars if her lawyers are successful. She doesn't have a criminal history and has always held a steady job. They'll take that into consideration when they sentence her."

"It's a pity," Clarence said, watching his friend pace. "If she and her half-brother didn't have the same shape and build, we would have plenty of witnesses that could place her behind May's Flower Shop, the scene of the crime, just hours before Horace died."

Jess stopped pacing and sat down at his desk. "It is uncanny how much they resemble each other. But even if we had witnesses, there's still the coroner's report ruling Gunther's cause of death a heart attack."

"But the report added that the heart attack was likely brought on by the fear of being assaulted. As he said, he was frightened to death. The ligatures on his neck show the intent."

"Yeah, I've always heard the term 'scared to death' but I didn't know it could actually happen."

"Even though the heart attack precipitated the murderer's intentions, don't forget about South Carolina's felony-murder rule. It says that a person can be charged with murder if he or she causes another person's death during the commission of a felony if malice is supplied from the intent to commit the underlying felony. It's pretty much a given that the person, whether it was Amelia or Balbini, was intending to steal the quilt from Gunther and that's a felony." He closed the folder in his lap and sighed. "But the fact that Gunther didn't have the quilt on his person changes things. It wasn't actually stolen because it wasn't there to steal. You're right. It would be a whole lot simpler if one of the witnesses could identify the hunched over figure in the raincoat as Amelia, because I also have a gut feeling she did it."

Jess jumped up from behind his desk almost turning his chair over, startling Clarence.

"Why didn't I think of it before! The raincoat!"

"What about the raincoat?"

"We have Amelia's possessions in the evidence room, don't we?" He could barely contain his excitement. "Did she have a raincoat?"

"Ahh," Clarence said, his own excitement building. "There was a raincoat. I'll race you to the basement."

"Just watch those steep stairs. I don't want you ending up in the hospital with a concussion, especially right before your wedding." He gave Clarence a friendly punch on the arm. "You old rascal. You blindsided me with that one."

"You're pretty dense if you didn't see it coming, Chief. It was written all over my face. I've been like a moonstruck puppy." He rushed out the door ahead of Jess. "Time's a-wastin'. Let's go pin some more charges on Amelia Reinhart. It'd be a crying shame if she got away with murder."

***

The witnesses on Main Street identified the raincoat that was found in Amelia's suitcase as the one worn by the stranger seen in town on the day of the murder. Horace's brown scarf, which both Valerie and Sam identified as the one he was wearing the day he came into the shop, was in the pocket of the raincoat. What more evidence could you ask for? And that's exactly what the jury thought when on the day of the trial, Amelia's face turned ashen when the scarf was pulled out of the pocket of her raincoat as evidence.

"Life in prison," Valerie said as she and Sam sat down with Jess and Clarence at the back booth of BJ's Diner after the sentencing was over. "I'm glad she didn't get the death penalty. Too many people have died already."

"I agree," Clarence said. "Maggie has already decided to donate the quilt to the Baltimore Museum of Art. She feels that her memories of her grandparents would be tainted if she kept it, what with all the tragic things that happened because of its value. The museum is where it belongs."

"And when is the wedding, Clarence? I was shocked, but happy at the same time when I heard the news. Sister M..., I mean Maggie is such a dear and sweet person."

He laughed. "That she is. And she realizes that it's going to be hard for the people she's met in Park Place to quit calling her Sister so don't worry about slipping up, Valerie. She was always called Maggie growing up and that's what she wants to be called now."

"We haven't known her so long that we can't relearn. It won't be so bad. But you didn't answer my question about the wedding?"

"Five weeks away, much too long for my liking. June 3rd is the actual date. She got word from the diocese just yesterday, so we haven't had a chance to send out invitations, but you'll get one soon. She wants the Sweet Tea Quilting Bee members to be there and of course Jess, Heather and Cliff. It will be at Park Place Presbyterian and Rev Rock will perform the ceremony. It will be simple ceremony so there will be no attendants, except for my granddaughter, the flower girl and my grandson, the ringbearer."

"So, your daughter is fine with your marriage?"

"Valerie!" Sam reached over and touched his wife's hand. "You're getting a little too personal with your questions, aren't you?"

"Oh, I'm sorry. I didn't mean to pry! Things just slip out of my mouth sometimes."

"That's okay," Clarence said. "Claire's happy for me. She's met Maggie and thinks I'm awfully lucky to have found her."

"Oh, I can't wait to tell the other quilters! I wish we had more time so we could make y'all a quilt for your wedding present."

Sam looked at his wife with affection. "Never mind her, Clarence. She's got quilting fever."

Valerie was lost in her own thoughts. "A June wedding. How romantic!" The three men laughed as she took a deep breath and sighed. "It's going to be so romantic."

CHAPTER 33

THE PERFECT GIFT

The Sweet Tea Quilting Bee quilters had been busy and now they had two major events on their calendar for the same week. The maternity wing of the hospital had been so thrilled with the quilt donations, the ladies had decided to continue making baby quilts until they had enough to cover all the cribs in the nursery. The sewing machines had been purring inside The Banty Hen. The hospital held a dedication ceremony on Monday. The Park Place Gazette, The Lancaster News and even The Charlotte Observer had covered the event. Even more exciting was the upcoming wedding ceremony of one of their own, Maggie Bayley to Clarence Foster on Saturday.

As a group, they had taken numerous shopping trips to find a perfect gift for Maggie and had slapped each other on the hand when they slipped up and called her Sister Margaret. They were beginning to despair of ever finding the right gift. They were discussing it at their weekly meeting, when the chimes on the front door sounded.

"Maybe that's Maggie," Maura said. "Was she coming in late?"

"I forgot to tell you," Valerie said. "Her parents came in last night and they're staying with Clarence. She won't be here today." Valerie heard Sam as he spoke with someone at the front counter. In a few minutes, he came to the room and stuck his head in the door.

"Valerie, can you come out here for just a moment? Our picker from Connecticut is here and he's got something I think you'll want to see."

"What is it, Sam? Will you bring it back here? If it's something nice, the ladies might want to see it."

"I'd love to see it," Maura said. A chorus of "me too's" followed.

Sam walked out and the group continued working on the quilt pieces they were cutting. The friendly chatter was all about the upcoming wedding. A few minutes later, Sam walked in with a cloth sack, that looked for all the world like an old pillowcase. "I've already seen it, but we put it back in here so you girls could get the full effect when I open it." He took the pillowcase by the corners and emptied it onto one of the tables.

"A quilt!" Valerie exclaimed.

"Not just any old quilt," Sam said. "Look at the design." As he unfolded it, beautiful appliqued squares came to life. A collective gasp was heard around the room. "Don't get too excited," he said. "It's not a genuine Baltimore Album Quilt made in the 1800's. It's a recent reproduction. The pattern is called *Ladies of the Sea*. I thought it such a coincidence that he brought it by now of all times. What do you think?"

Valerie could barely breathe. Were the others thinking what she was thinking. She hesitated to ask, but she did anyway. "How much?", then she held her breath waiting for the answer.

Sam looked around at the small statured man standing behind him. "You see these lovely ladies, Frank? They want to know how much for the quilt."

Frank looked at Valerie and smiled. "Do you like it, Valerie?"

"It's beautiful. I love it. I have something in mind..." She looked around at the other women. "But I need to know the cost."

"For you, $700, and I'm not making any more than my travel expenses on it. Of course, I'm counting on you guys to buy a good bit of my inventory...." He grinned.

"We always do," she said. "And that's a fair price, Frank." She wasn't sure what to say. She couldn't speak for the others.

"Sold!" It was Madge Price. "It's the perfect wedding gift for Maggie, and if any of you can't afford your share, I'll pay it. At my age, I've got more money than I can ever spend anyway." The others all laughed and the gift for Maggie was settled.

***

The first three rows on each side of the aisle of Park Place Presbyterian were filled. Cliff was the one and only usher and he refused to let anyone be a backseater, dragging them to the front of the church by the lapel of their jackets if necessary, but no one much minded. The Sweet Tea Quilting Bee members were all present, along with their husbands. The Park Place Police Department was out in full force, all three of them, plus Cliff's wife and Rebecca Hamilton. Vic and Nancy Battles, Clarence's neighbors who had first invited him and Teresa to church were there, glad to see happiness in the eyes of their friend once again.

Maggie's mother and stepfather were there on the front seat, happy for their daughter who was stepping out in faith to begin a new phase of her life. Clarence's daughter and son-in-law were sitting across the aisle on the front seat, nervously awaiting their children's trek down the aisle, one to scatter flowers and the other to hold the rings. Four-year-old Rance had already lost the rings tucked inside the cushion once at practice, but they had finally shown up in his pocket along with a lizard that jumped out and almost gave Rev Rock a heart attack. His wife, Liz laughed so hard, she cried, saying it was an inside joke.

Somehow Betty from the post office got wind of it and there she was, uninvited but welcome, sitting beside May from the flower shop who said if she was going to dress up the church with flowers, she was surely going to be there to see how they held up for the wedding.

Clarence stood at the front with Rock as Jenny Wilson began to play the Wedding March on the organ, and smiled broadly as he watched Father Thomas lead his beautiful Maggie down the aisle.

When they reached the front, a hush fell over the crowd and Rev Rock's voice boomed out, "Who presents this woman to be married to this man?"

Father Thomas, with a big grin on his face made his own voice boom out loudly to match Rev Rock's. "Her Mother Superior and I!"

Laughter is good for the soul and it could be heard ringing off the rafters and down the aisles of Park Place Presbyterian on that exquisite June afternoon.

The End

OTHER BOOKS BY THIS AUTHOR:

- Sweet Tea and Southern Grace
- Lighting the Way
- High Tide at Pelican Point
- The Melancholy Moon

Made in the USA
Coppell, TX
27 February 2024